The shadows of the flames from the fireplace danced against the walls, interspersing with the patter of rain hitting his windows. Tony switched on the radio and settled back in his chair. Seconds later, he heard her voice.

"Just a voice in the night to tell you you're not alone. This is Vee Matthews on the air with you until sunrise. Let's embrace this rainy night with Etta James…"

What did she look like? It didn't really matter. Her voice was calm and soothing, and her playlist similar to the DJ she was temporarily replacing.

Several hours later he woke with a start to the sound of thunder. The storm was still a distance away. With the next streak of lightning, he started counting. When he reached eleven, he smiled to himself as the thunder rumbled in the background. He moved to stretch out on the couch, comforted by her voice.

I0598276

**Cheryl A. Cornell's Previous Releases
with The Wild Rose Press**

A LITTLE COLOR IN HIS LIFE
which received a 5-Book Rating from Long and Short
Reviews and was an All Romance eBook favorite
THE PROXY WIFE
ANOTHER MAN'S LOVE
WHAT THE HEART HEARS

Hiding in Plain Sight

by

Cheryl A. Cornell

This is a work of fiction. Names, characters, places, and incidents are either the product of the author's imagination or are used fictitiously, and any resemblance to actual persons living or dead, business establishments, events, or locales, is entirely coincidental.

Hiding in Plain Sight

COPYRIGHT © 2020 by Cheryl A. Cornell

All rights reserved. No part of this book may be used or reproduced in any manner whatsoever without written permission of the author or The Wild Rose Press, Inc. except in the case of brief quotations embodied in critical articles or reviews.
Contact Information: info@thewildrosepress.com

Cover Art by *Tina Lynn Stout*

The Wild Rose Press, Inc.
PO Box 708
Adams Basin, NY 14410-0708
Visit us at www.thewildrosepress.com

Publishing History:
Previously published by Red Rose Publishing, 2009
First Crimson Rose Edition, 2020
Trade Paperback ISBN 978-1-5092-2966-6
Digital ISBN 978-1-5092-2967-3

Published in the United States of America

Dedication

To all who serve and protect

Acknowledgments

My thanks to everyone at The Wild Rose Press
for their continued support,
especially my very patient editor,
Roseann Armstrong,
and to
Tina Lynn Stout for the beautiful cover art.

Chapter One

Tony shifted the plastic-covered bag of dry cleaning he was holding as well as the plastic bag with beer and ice cream and tucked his unread newspaper under his arm. He let out an exasperated sigh as he read the sign telling him the elevator was once again out of order. He moved to the bottom of the staircase and looked up. He took a moment to open the snaps on his down jacket and debated taking it off. He didn't when he realized he'd only have to carry it too.

He took the first flight two steps at a time. On the second-floor landing, a scent assaulted him, and he took only shallow breaths as he moved quickly through the landing and up the third and fourth flights of stairs. The smell lost its power there, and he breathed normally again. He wasn't sure what the odor was and chatted often with Gus, the daytime doorman, about it. It wasn't offensive like someone cooking cabbage. It was more of a dense perfume smell that seemed to go stale. He could only liken it to a funeral home. It gave him the creeps each time he smelled it. Nothing he could put his finger on, but the hairs standing on the back of his neck made him uneasy.

The thought lingered as he opened the last lock on his door and hit the appropriate numbers on the alarm keypad. Inside, he repeated the process in reverse. He hung his cleaning and jacket on the hallstand and dropped his newspaper on the seat of the old leather chair beside the gas fireplace. He pulled the string on the floor lamp behind the chair, illuminating the living room around him. With a turn of the knob, the gas flames leaped to life, instantly warming the immediate area around him.

He put five of the green bottles of imported beer in the refrigerator. Then he paused to pull out a frozen pizza, replaced it with the ice cream, and preheated the oven while fighting with the plastic wrapping. He dropped it onto the rack before heading toward the bedroom.

Stripping along the way, he thought it was odd he had no messages. Not a good sign. It was too calm, too quiet. That usually meant the other shoe was about to drop. For tonight, he hoped it would drop on somebody else. He showered and decided that since he had spent most of the day yesterday in Brooklyn with his family, there probably wasn't anything new going on. He pulled his bathrobe belt tighter against the chill in the room. Draining the last of the warm beer, he headed back to the kitchen. The pizza was hot, and the cheese bubbling. He managed to get it out without burning himself and dropped it onto a plate to cool.

With another cold beer and the plate in hand, he went back to the living room and ate his supper before the fire. Once he was full and the dish washed, he settled back in the chair to relax. The rain pelted the windows in a fury. It had started after nine, and he was just thankful it held off long enough to get home.

By midnight, his belly was full, and his eyes bleary from reading the newspaper. Something about the feel of the paper and the ink on his fingers made him feel alive. While he could have read the same news on his tablet or laptop, he preferred the paper version. He'd spent a few minutes trying to read the new thriller he'd downloaded on the tablet. He hadn't gotten time to read it yet, but it wouldn't keep his attention tonight either. He stretched behind him to turn off the light. The shadows of the flames from the fireplace danced against the walls, interspersing with the patter of rain hitting his windows. Tony switched on the radio and settled back in his chair. Seconds later, he heard her voice.

"Just a voice in the night to tell you you're not alone. This is Vee Matthews on the air with you until sunrise. Let's embrace this rainy night with Etta James…"

What did she look like? It didn't really matter. Her voice was calm and soothing, and her playlist similar to the DJ she was temporarily replacing.

Several hours later he woke with a start to the sound of thunder. The storm was still a distance away. With the next streak of lightning, he started counting. When he reached eleven, he smiled to himself as the thunder rumbled in the background. He moved to stretch out on the couch, comforted by her voice.

"It's just after four, and the storm is still raging. Let's give an ear to…"

He dozed off again but woke with a stiff neck when his alarm squealed at six forty-five. All but falling off the couch, he stumbled to the bedroom and slammed the clock radio off. The beeping stopped, but it had done its job. He was awake, and he wouldn't sleep again. He pulled on his sweatpants for warmth before he made his way to the kitchen and flipped the switch on his ever-ready coffee maker.

No matter how late or hurried, he always made a point of setting up the coffee pot, having learned that he didn't have the patience to take the extra time when he wanted his coffee. Waiting for it to brew took long enough. After detouring to the front door, he went through the process of unlocking it and reached for his newspaper. This was his usual routine, except he wasn't prepared for the drowned person trying to get in the apartment across the hall. He was staring but couldn't stop himself.

With wet hair plastered to her face and neck and eye makeup pooling in dark circles under her eyes, she was quite a sight. He knew he surprised her from the swift intake of air he heard rushing into her lungs and the defensive stance her body spun into. The keys fell from her hands and clanked as they hit the floor. She bent to retrieve them, then froze when her gaze met his.

****

Home—such a simple word with so many different meanings to different people. The idea that she had one again was almost overwhelming sometimes, especially the feeling Vaughn got every time she came back to this beautiful building and this new apartment. Even the hateful rain didn't diminish the well-being that came over her each time she arrived home.

She hated storms. They were the one holdover—all right, maybe one of a few holdovers—from the last eight years. Rainstorms she could handle, but thunder shook her to the core. The lightning reminded her of the light glinting off the knife as it made a cold streak across her skin. Automatically, her hand went to her throat, which was covered in a wet cotton turtleneck sweater.

4

She watched the stranger intently, as intently as he watched her. Judging by his height in the doorway, he was tall. His upper body was bare, his chest spreading into wide shoulders and melding down into a flat stomach. His arms looked strong and muscled, his hands large, and his fingers thick and long with neat nails but no rings. She couldn't help but notice the dark, curling hairs covering his chest and running in a straight pattern down under the waistband of his sweatpants. He hadn't bothered to cinch up the belt on his robe. He was barefoot.

Only after overtly sizing him up did she let her eyes wander to his face, her breath catching in her throat. He was dark skinned with darker hair that brushed the back of his neck and looked as if he'd just gotten up. His eyes were dark too, but they weren't menacing. Several gray strands of hair had found their way to his temples and mixed with short sideburns. He smiled at her, and she knew she was in trouble. Her frozen wet skin went warm with a heat she hadn't felt in years, warmth she wasn't comfortable with.

"It's raining," she said, instantly realizing how lame it sounded.

His smile widened as he nodded. "Does that sometimes." His voice was deep and confident, with a hint of laughter.

Straight, white teeth presented themselves from behind soft-looking lips, and she wondered if he was a good kisser. Heat coursed up her throat and landed on her cheeks. She forced herself to reach down and find her keys, her gaze not leaving his.

"Do you live here?" The question slid from her lips before she could pull it back. "I mean, you could be visiting or…something." Her cheeks heated further from embarrassment, and she managed to turn away and fit the key into the second lock. When she turned back, he was leaning in the doorway, still watching her.

"Anthony Lombardo the Fifth," he told her. "Everybody calls me Tony." His gaze glanced over her one more time, assessing her. He did it openly, and she felt the same tingle deep inside her for a second time.

"I'm new…to the building. Nice to have met you, Mr. Lombardo…Tony." She moved to block the view of her alarm keypad and punched in a long list of numbers. The alarm beeped, and she pushed open her door. She paused and gave him one last look, hoping he wouldn't recognize the longing on her face. Uneasy with the personal acknowledgment, she slid inside.

She repeated the process in reverse, using the back of the door to support her weight when she was inside. She stood for several moments, waiting for her breath to return to normal. This just wouldn't do. Her long coat left a full circle of water at her feet, and she trudged through the apartment to the bathroom and stripped.

She'd gotten off her coat and scarf, dropping both on the tile floor beside the reproduction claw-foot bathtub she was so fond of, and fought with herself to strip off the rest of her wet things and flip on the shower. She pulled a large, unfeminine terry-cloth robe from the hook on the inside of the door and struggled to wrap herself in it before she returned to the living room.

She surveyed each room with a practiced eye until she was comfortable everything was in its place. She stopped to check her booby traps and found them all intact. Each time she entered this space, a peaceful feeling swept through her. The colors created the warmth she felt. The deep apricot she'd had the walls painted reflected the early morning light trying to peek through the storm clouds. The glossy, white trim glowed back, unmarred by fingerprints. She breathed a sigh of relief.

In the bedroom, she paused to check the large paper clips she'd placed on top of the doors. Relief flowed over her as she found them exactly as she'd left them. One more test and she would relax. The single long, dark hair she'd laid across the top of the clothes in her oak bureau was still in place.

Vaughn turned up the volume on the flat-screen television she'd had mounted in the far corner. It was never turned off; she'd only turned the volume down or up depending on her mood. This morning she grabbed the remote and listened to the early morning news. It was the same as what she'd been telling her listeners all night, but it didn't matter. She wasn't alone. A human voice was with her, and that was all that mattered. She wasn't alone.

She paused to test the water before stepping under it, then dropped the robe and glanced into the foggy mirror over the sink. A gasp escaped her as she took in her plastered hair and dripping makeup. The dark circles of mascara under her eyes had given way to several long streaks that dripped down her cheeks. Laughing at the sight of herself, she dismissed any notions of what her new neighbor must think of her. It made her smile, finally allowing her to enjoy the warmth of the water sluicing around her.

"Serves you right." Running across town in a storm had been crazy. She should have waited for a cab, but the storm shook her. Her only goal had been to get home where she felt safe.

After her bath, she entered the kitchen. The painters had double-checked her color choice, but she hadn't cared. She'd spent enough time in nondescript rooms to last her a lifetime. The turquoise and yellow ceramic tiles on the counters and backsplash comforted her. Though they were all brand new, her authentic reproduction appliances gave the room a feel as if it had been born in the nineteen fifties.

The Formica table with the metal-frame chairs fitted with yellow vinyl pads stood empty, waiting for her to take a seat. She popped a bagel in the toaster and waited until the kettle whistled its readiness to be poured over the Earl Grey bag already placed in her favorite mug. As soon as it finished toasting, she slathered cream cheese on the bagel she'd stopped for on the way home. The bagel was her only concession to the storm.

She forced herself to take the meal to the table and sit to eat. This was a new start, and she refused to conform to old habits. Sitting and eating like a normal human was important. The days of standing over the sink and gobbling down her food were long gone. The news show droned on in the background, the anchors friendly with a little too much spunk for seven in the morning.

She cleaned up and took her second cup of tea in hand. With her hair still wrapped in a towel, Vaughn forced herself to the bedroom window. Standing several feet away, she waited for the next assault of thunder. She didn't have to wait long. Even though she was prepared for it, she still jumped. The television continued to drone on. She grabbed the remote and turned up the volume, then tossed the remote toward the pillows. Sitting straight-backed on the foot of her bed, she waited for the half-hour weather update. She unwrapped her hair and used the time to comb out the tangles.

Just as she'd known, it was going to storm all day. She pulled back the silk comforter and dropped between the cool sheets, the down covering her in a glove of warmth. She snaked a hand out from under the covers and upped the volume. Deep breaths allowed her to relax in the shell of pillows and blankets. She drifted off to sleep with a strange smile on her lips, a smile induced by the thought of Anthony Lombardo the Fifth.

****

Tony couldn't concentrate on his newspaper, so he tossed it aside. He was on his fourth cup of coffee and behind schedule because he was thinking about his new neighbor. Maybe it was the cop in him, but it hadn't eluded him that she didn't introduce herself. In fact, she'd managed to avoid it quite smoothly. What had her reaction been when she realized she looked like a drowned raccoon? Somehow, he didn't think it would bother her, and that intrigued him.

Gus held the umbrella over Tony's head as he ran the distance from the canopied entrance to the waiting cab. With a nod of thanks, he rambled off the street address of the old city hall to the cabdriver. Because he'd be spending the day in the archives, he hadn't minded the storm. If he was going to waste a day in a dank room filled with musty old papers, it might as well be a rainy day. His gaze took in the city coming to life around him, mass quantities of people all trying to get somewhere at the same time.

Twice a day, five days a week, the same thing happened. Yet on rainy days he always was a bit depressed by the shift of humans. Maybe it was the rain-soaked window he watched through. While he was thankful for the protection, the window distanced him from it all, just as he distanced himself from the rest of the world. He wasn't antisocial by any means. What little spare time he had, he wanted to do what he wanted to do.

Twenty years of his life had passed him in what seemed like a few breaths. Now he wanted to use time for his own purposes. His new life suited him just fine. He was getting accustomed to the nonroutine of his routine and learning how to make the most of his time. It was a simple matter of mathematics. He had twenty-four hours a day to work with. He had to take that time and divide it by the obligations of daily life, professional and personal. Subtract travel, errands, and build in a fail-safe for the unknowns, especially travel-time glitches, and what was left was his downtime.

Time was the first thing that came to his mind when he awoke from the shooting. Not was he or was his partner all right. No, he'd come awake in a mass of pain and thought of all the time he promised he'd give himself one day. Life as he'd known it was gone in a flash that he couldn't control, making his job seem pointless. He'd spent most of his adult life behaving the way society taught him, and for what? To be shot by some punk kid with a loaded gun in a botched robbery. It didn't even out. Realizing how lucky he'd been up until then, he easily walked away. Retirement felt right.

This time, the next phase of his life was for him to

discover who he truly was. He'd just turned forty-five, never married, only came close once. The image of Alyssa's face materialized on the inside of his closed eyes. She was beautiful and laughed a lot. She hated her baby-fine blonde hair, but he loved the color. Her blue eyes always smiled at him, no matter how badly one of their jobs interfered with their precious time together.

She was the only female friend he truly cared for. They understood each other and didn't hold any grudges from their past. They managed to get in a monthly email these days, and every few months one of them would initiate a telephone call. She was happy in her new life, and he was learning what made him happy in his.

He was roused from his thoughts by the sound of a car horn coming dangerously close to his side of the cab. The cab swayed and tossed him across the seat. Straightening, he realized he was only a few blocks from his destination and sent up a silent prayer. He paid the driver without comment. His umbrella took the brunt of the rain while he walked into the building.

Why had he been thinking about Alyssa? It somehow had to do with his wet neighbor. The few words she'd spoken went to his core, as if they'd met before. But they hadn't. He had an uncanny ability to remember faces and voices. Though he'd never seen her, he'd heard her before.

The deep rasp in her voice, he decided, was from too many cigarettes. Yet it didn't fit her. The whole subject was starting to get on his nerves as he presented his identification and signed in. Then he handed over his briefcase to be checked. Only after clearing the metal detectors did he let his mind wander to the purpose he'd come for.

Tony greeted several people he knew before escaping the crowded halls to the dark depths of the archives. There, only dust motes presented problems. And of course, the lost information he was looking for.

****

Gus was just going off duty when Tony arrived home. He timed it to look coincidental, but it was carefully arranged. He greeted Patrick as he came on shift, and the three of them debated the weather. He dropped a suggestion that a short whiskey might warm his bones and ten minutes later was sitting at the bar around the corner. Gus was out of uniform, and a cold beer sat before him. It matched the one Tony had wrapped his hand around. It wasn't unusual for them to share a beer after Gus's shift ended.

Since his retirement, they usually managed to have a beer or two once a month. Gus was the most well-informed man in the building and its neighboring ones, and he knew all their naughty little secrets. They'd met at the bar occasionally in the first few years after Tony moved in, but his hours had been erratic until he'd formally retired. Now he enjoyed knowing what was going on around him and gave a rueful laugh at the concept that he'd become a second-hand voyeur of sorts.

Tonight he had an agenda, and it was time to get down to business. After clearing his throat, he took a long pull from his mug, only to turn and see a big grin on Gus's ruddy cheeks. He placed the glass back on the bar in front of him with a shake of his head. "That transparent?"

"I figured you were about due. She's been in the

building for two weeks." Gus followed the path of a large drip of condensation that ran down the outside of his glass with a short, stubby index finger.

"All right, I give. I just met her."

"And?" Gus drank from his glass before answering his own question. "Don't know much. She's quiet and keeps to herself. Works nights. Doing what, I don't know." His tone wasn't judgmental, just informative. "Remember a while back we were talking about a new tenant that was doing the whole renovation over the internet? That was her."

"And?" Tony parroted.

"And I don't know much more. She's a looker. First day here she introduced herself to me, thanked me for helping the contractor get his work done, pleasant and friendly yet remote. It's like she doesn't want to let anybody near her. Sad eyes," Gus whispered.

Tony tilted his glass against his. "That she has."

They were quiet for a while, though the noise of the bar grew louder with each wave of people coming through the door.

"I'll tell you this because I trust you." He waited until Tony nodded his never-heard-it-from-Gus look. "She's got one tough security system up there. It's got a twelve-digit code and a fingerprint ID backup. Hell, I wouldn't be surprised if it had an iris scanner too. Had a private security firm come in and set up the place. Big bucks! Lots of private security while the renovation was going on too. You were on vacation when most of that was happening. Even had the feds in here one day just before she moved in."

Tony acknowledged the significance of the information. He prided himself on security, and he only had an eight-digit code. He stewed over the information before he changed the subject. "Want to grab a table before it gets too crowded?"

They gave their orders to the bartender and took their newly filled glasses to a far corner table. They shared other bits of information over their burgers with thick-cut fries—from football to Tony's sister's kids, from Gus's grandson who had no athletic ability to the newly married couple on the third floor and their many overnight guests.

Tony himself had gotten in the small compartment of the elevator with them one evening and was taken aback by their amorous touching. He'd relayed the tidbit to Gus one night, who'd confided he always took the service elevator if they were around.

"To being young and in love," Tony toasted.

"To the body being capable," Gus toasted back, his free hand rubbing his full belly.

They stood shoulder to shoulder, buttoning up coats and opening umbrellas, just outside the bar. Gus would turn right toward home, and Tony would walk to the apartment building just around the corner. He'd be home in no time, but he'd be wet no matter what.

"See ya tomorrow, Tony."

"Yeah, Gus, you too. Say hi to Marge for me." He nodded but didn't move away, putting his free hand in his coat pocket and waiting.

After a protracted silence, Gus finally spoke. "Never takes the elevator, always the stairs." He waited while Tony absorbed the information. "Probably the only exercise she gets in a day."

"Probably…"

"Night, Tony." Gus moved to the right into the

cold drizzle of rain still falling from the darkened sky.

Tony contemplated this new information on his walk home. She probably had a desk job. Or maybe she was afraid of elevators? Or maybe just claustrophobic? Or maybe she was just afraid? He thanked Patrick for holding the door while he shook out and closed his umbrella and hesitated before pushing the button for the elevator. Then he changed his mind.

Tonight he unbuttoned his coat and took the stairs two at a time, jogging through the landing on the second floor. When he reached the top, he paused and leaned on the railing. Looking down, he saw the same thing he'd seen the first day he viewed his apartment— the large open square of the stairway left the lower lobby visible from all floors. Nobody could hide behind the ornate scrollwork railings.

The stairs came up on each floor in the far corner. One long hall separated the apartments. A person had full view of the corridor before he committed himself to the hallway. He walked to his door, acknowledging the way the apartment doors were staggered. Each door opened to the wall, not to another apartment door. It was as safe and secure as you could get in a renovated Manhattan apartment building.

Standing before his door, he glanced across to hers. It was the last one on her side. That meant she had the mirror image of his apartment. Only the hallways would be different. They both had bedrooms overlooking the city street. An interesting tidbit he'd filed away long ago when he was being nosy during the start of her renovation. He'd seen workmen come and go with outrageous colors of paint and tile. His curiosity had gotten the better of him, and he'd hovered in the doorway one afternoon. Then he'd gone on vacation. He shook his head, likening the colors to chaos.

He locked himself in his apartment and was oddly relieved when he had several nonsense messages to deal with. He managed to stay busy until eleven. He watched the early news, showered, and stretched out in his bed, listening to a comic's monologue. He fidgeted with the remote in his hand, snapping off the television before the first guest came on to be interviewed. Padding naked across his carpeted room, he flipped on the stereo just in time to hear the words he'd waited for. He took that remote with him back to bed.

"Just a voice in the night to tell you you're not alone. Tonight I'm in the mood to be blue for a while. I suppose it's all this rain. Let's start with..."

He closed his eyes, the song lulling him to sleep. He woke with a start and realized his alarm was ringing. He pulled himself up against the headboard and then used the heels of his hands to scrub the sleep from his eyes. It had happened again. He'd slept through the night. Several nights in the past few weeks, he'd slept through the night like a normal person, the sleep of the dead. He was used to making do with a few hours caught when he could and several catnaps when he could fit them in.

The crazy part was he'd begun to associate the nights he slept with the nights Vee Matthews had been on the air. Tonight he'd skip the radio show just to prove to himself it was all a fluke of timing. He'd finally settled into his new life and was adjusting. Wasn't this one of the things he hoped for? To be able to sleep at night and leave the world outside his door?

So why was he questioning it when it finally happened?

Because he knew it was since the new DJ had taken over his favorite radio station he'd begun to sleep. The idea kept chasing around in his mind while he showered and dressed. Today was going to be an instant replay of yesterday, still wet but the rain much lighter. His destination would be the same.

Chapter Two

Vaughn managed to keep her emotions steady when she emerged from the soundproof booth and found it was still raining. Thankfully, the thunder and lightning had stopped. Rain she could conquer, so she easily accepted a breakfast offer from her boss, Albert. He managed the station as if it were his sacred trust. She'd interviewed for the job mostly by telephone and then video conferences. She was still in Seattle, doing voice-over work and fill-in shifts at a small public station. While mostly relaying the news and weather reports, she got to program a few hours of each shift. That was when she found the blues, or it found her, being a matter of what was available for her to play. But she liked the job, liked learning how to manipulate the sounds and programs. Liked the feeling of control it gave her.

It also opened up a new door for her in a different direction. On the radio, she could be heard but not seen. She liked the anonymity in the situation. When she was finally healed from her last surgery and ready to move forward with her life, Jacob had given her the idea of sending her demo tapes to stations across the country. She'd received three offers.

One was to stay in the Seattle area, but she had to move on. Staying in Seattle was too safe. It was time to go back into the world, or she might never get there.

The station in Austin was just too close to home, her long-lost home. She could never go back to Texas. So when Albert called her from the small and struggling blues-slash-jazz-formatted station in New York, she wanted the job. But she made several uncommon requests.

First, she would only come to Manhattan once, for the final meeting and to sign her contract. Second, no photographs were to be used for any station purpose, especially advertising or promotion. She was to remain a simple voice she hoped comforted those who listened.

Albert might have thought her strange and backed away, but he told her that when they finally met, the eccentricities she showed were dismissed by the sincerity he heard in her voice. He also shared that even his jaded teenaged son had been impressed by her tape. Apparently, he hadn't had a decent conversation with the boy since he hit his teens. He'd offered a door to friendship, and she was slowly walking toward it. Once they'd met, she liked his wife, Nancy, and his son, Eric.

None of them looked like what she pictured, but that was okay too. She never knew what people expected from her these days. She wasn't sure what to expect of herself, only that she remained self-sufficient and alive. Who she turned into would come with time. Nancy joined them for breakfast before going off to her accounting job for a firm in the same building.

Vaughn even managed to get a cab home this morning, snagging one from an executive-looking man on his way to work in her building. She'd seen him before and nodded as he held the door for her. She'd also been observant enough to note he wore a gold ring on his third left finger. He was polite but married. Good for him. She liked him, even though she didn't know him, because he never leered. Maybe she wasn't his type, but she liked her version of a happily married man better.

She smiled at Gus as he held open the door, but she didn't linger in conversation. Since she had breakfast out, she was later than usual getting home. Pausing at the bottom of the staircase, she traced each flight with a quick eye. No flashes of color or movement had her taking them at an easy pace. She held her breath at the heavy floral odor on the second-floor landing and moved easily up the next two flights.

Halfway up, she moved her keys to position the first one between her thumb and index finger. The hall was empty, and she drew a breath and headed for her door. The first lock snapped. As she reached for the second, a door shutting behind her made her bolt upright, her shoulders snapping back and her body tensing. She glanced behind her and saw him, Anthony Lombardo, coming through the doorway.

This morning his dark hair was combed, but she'd been right. He was in severe need of a trim. The bulky down jacket he wore covered his upper body, exposing only strong-looking thighs encased in denim. His legs were long, and she remembered how he fitted his doorway yesterday morning.

He caught sight of her as he opened his door, paused, and seemed to decide something. Finally, he smiled in her direction before turning his attention back to his task. "Good morning."

"Morning," Vaughn managed to whisper.

He must have heard her because he acknowledged her with a nod before walking away. Only when he disappeared down the first few stairs did she let her body relax against the door.

****

She hadn't seen him peeking through the railing, watching her. When she was inside, Tony turned and went the rest of the way down. He felt his lips curl into a snarky smile but couldn't define why. Somehow, he knew their meetings made her nervous. The smile disappeared when he realized it could be men in general that caused her discomfort. The possibilities of why were staggering, so he decided not to try and figure it out blind.

He had work to do, and a young woman's future might depend on what he could dig up. With that firmly in mind, he went to work, his dark-haired neighbor neatly positioned in the rear of his brain, almost. She'd been dry today, and that was worse. He was able to see how beautiful she really was.

Her dark brown hair fluffed around her shoulders. It had red highlights when the light caught it just right. Her eyes were brown, as he'd decided yesterday, but still as sad even without the dark circles. She was on alert. Maybe she was new to Manhattan and was acting in defense of everything bad anyone had ever told her about the place. Or maybe she was "hiding in plain sight," as the old saying went.

Today he was going back to his old station. He'd see several of the men he used to work with and hopefully grab a computer station for a half hour without anyone noticing. He could access the same data from his own elaborate computer setup, but he didn't want it to be traced back. It was one less loose end, and he hated loose ends. They tended to unravel when tugged on. That was how he'd solved so many cases in his career. He never let the little details slip away.

****

Two weeks had gone by, and Tony was no closer to finding the truth about Danielle Rimon-Aubin than any of the other investigators had been. She'd literally disappeared after leaving work one Thursday evening in 2010. Her husband had been the one to report her missing and at the time had impressed the investigating officers of his sincerity. While they had checked him out thoroughly, his alibi had stood. There was a full basketball court, not to mention the parents, teachers, and students who swore he was there the entire time. Several cell-phone videos provided proof.

Danielle had been accounted for up until four that afternoon. Her coworkers said she seemed fine, the same sweet, laughing woman they all knew. No one had ever heard her utter a bad word about her family and especially her husband. It was after eight that night when George Aubin had gone home and found her missing. He'd called her parents and friends, but no one was sure of her whereabouts.

The authorities had suspected him of foul play but never produced any evidence to prove their theories. He'd been at the high school all day and coached the basketball team to victory that evening. He'd been under surveillance on and off for years because the Rimon family had not been able to accept that their daughter's disappearance had nothing to do with him.

Her car had never been found, and no trace of Danielle ever turned up. There was no activity on her credit cards, and her private accounts were never touched. Neither were they able to find where she'd hidden funds if she'd decided to run on her own. She simply disappeared one day.

All these years later, George Aubin had the audacity to get engaged to another woman, a woman the Rimons thought looked suspiciously like their long-lost daughter. They had contacted Tony through a lawyer who knew of him. He'd said he'd read their case but wouldn't guarantee any results or that he'd even look into it.

Pushing back in the swivel chair at the old drafting table he used as a workspace, he dropped his reading glasses on the papers. He glanced at the wall clock as he turned on the radio. She was well past her intro, and he only half listened to the songs as they played.

He dropped his head to the table, his eyes closing automatically. His neck protested the position, but he stayed there anyway, thinking about his new neighbor. He'd seen her several times in passing, one of them leaving or coming. She was always polite but definitely couldn't be considered chatty. She would nod and smile, say "morning" or "evening," and slip away.

They had been neighbors for a while, and he still didn't know her name. Gus hadn't dropped it, and he hadn't come right out and asked. He figured he'd be able to get it from her mailbox. Hers was the only one blatantly absent of the small black-tape label announcing her name over the bank of mailboxes in the lobby. By the time he decided to look, Gus had gone on vacation. He'd be back next Monday, and he would find out. He didn't want to talk to the other doormen. They were fine men. He just didn't have the same trust relationship with them that he had with Gus.

He forced himself to shut down the computer and

dropped on the top of the bed. Pulling up the covers was too much of an effort. He dreamed of a dark-haired woman running through fog. The dream made no sense when he woke in a sweat. He remembered it completely and tried to analyze it while chugging cold milk from the plastic carton. Nothing made sense. Was he dreaming about Danielle? Or his nameless neighbor? Or was he dreaming about the mysterious Vee Matthews from his radio listening?

Shaking his head, he glanced at the clock. It was just past four. With an instant decision, he jogged back to his bedroom, turned on the shower, and pulled his old leather satchel from the inner depths of his closet. He threw back the cover, hoping not to find an assortment of dirty laundry long forgotten from his last trip.

"Empty." He sighed with relief.

After record time in the shower, he dragged on clothes while tossing spares into the bag. He paused long enough to fill two travel cups with hot coffee and made sure he stuffed the Rimon-Aubin file in his computer case.

He slipped out into the early morning, ready to do battle with the parking attendant at the garage. He'd called earlier and only gotten their machine. He left a message telling them he needed his SUV brought around as soon as possible. Tony was more surprised when it was brought up just twenty minutes later. The roads were starting to fill with early-morning commuters.

He stopped just through the tunnel at the first gas station on the New Jersey turnpike and refilled his gas tank and coffee supply. He was halfway to Philadelphia before he voice activated his phone and let his parents know he was going out of town for a few days. At his age it was a ridiculous habit, but why make them worry? His mother had spent the better part of her adult life wondering and worrying about her family—first, her policeman husband, then her cop son, and still her patrolman son-in-law. She thanked him for letting her know and wished him well on his fact-finding expedition.

****

The check Vaughn just deposited made her smile. The voice-overs she'd done on the automobile commercial had been a success. Today she'd done three more in the series. She swelled with pride that she could earn her own money again. Between her job with the station and picking up daywork occasionally, she was finding life was treating her well.

Today she even managed to get in a telephone call to her parents. She'd gone downtown and used a telephone she was promised was untraceable. Her parents sounded upbeat, and she was able to report that she was enjoying her work and her new home. The thought of her new home made her realize she hadn't seen Tony Lombardo the Fifth for a while, and the fact that she thought about him made her pause. She allowed herself to enjoy the concept that one day she might meet the right man and form a relationship but not yet. She had to be self-sufficient before relying on anyone else.

Her parents knew the home part was what really counted to their Vivian. Her mother had slipped and called her Viv today. She smiled at the face she knew her father would have flashed her mother as soon as the old name passed her lips. It was a matter of adjustment for all of them.

****

It was warm for a January day, and Vaughn almost forgot to be afraid walking the crowded city streets. She had an early supper at a little Italian place she'd found on Lexington. They were friendly but usually allowed her privacy to read the book she always brought with her while she dined alone. There had been times when she wouldn't have believed this simple act could become reality.

She'd started having breakfast at a little grill near her station. Armed with a newspaper, she was no different from many of the early-morning diners. It had broken her fear of the mundane act. Now she treated herself to supper out twice a week, but always with a book in hand and always as soon as the doors opened. By the time she was sated with rich food and her one glass of burgundy, the restaurant would be filling.

She had tonight off, and she almost felt let down. Anyone else would relish the two nights off each week. For her, the downtime threw her off schedule. She laughed to herself as she hit the landing of the fourth floor. She paused when she saw a shape in the hallway and then realized it was Anthony Lombardo the Fifth, a battered suitcase on the floor beside him.

He'd glanced at the stairs when she turned the corner, but she would have felt stupid turning around and heading back down. She took a deep breath and slowly made her way along the hall. By the time she reached him, he was pulling the case inside his apartment. He nodded to her as she passed, closing his door.

****

Tony was thankful to be home from his nonproductive work trip and about to relock himself in when he heard a scream. He tripped over the suitcase lying just inside his door. His alarm wailed in the process, but he didn't care. Standing in the hallway in front of her apartment, his neighbor seemed frozen in fear. He glanced down the hallway, but it was empty. Scattered about her feet was a broken vase, shards of glass all around her.

He stopped long enough to shut off his alarm before going to her. She didn't acknowledge him approaching. Carefully and most of all quietly, he moved toward her.

"Are you all right?" he asked in as soothing a voice as he could manage. "Are you hurt?" He moved closer with each question. His foot caught on something round, and he almost lost his balance. He glanced down to see the hall littered with dozens of clear marbles and what must have been a quart of water. The flowers were in a disheveled pile at her feet, interspersed with broken glass. He advanced closer, still asking her if she was all right.

When he reached her, he was quiet. Her eyes were wide, and her pupils fixed. He'd seen people in shock before, and she certainly fit the criteria. He reached a hand toward her. "It's all right. Come with me, away from the broken glass." His hand stayed twelve inches in front of her. He knew better than to grab. "Come on. It will be fine. Just be careful of the glass and the water." He waited and tried again.

She'd blinked a few times, but her body was still rigid, her eyes still wide. In her hand she held a small white card.

"Really, I'm a klutz sometimes too. Come with me, and we'll clean up this mess."

She still didn't acknowledge his presence. He edged closer, then stopped when she looked at him. "It's all right. Just be careful of the broken glass." He continued to use a calm voice. "Come on. Be careful. The floor's wet."

He held out his hand to her again, and she looked at it, then back to him and back to his hand. Whatever had happened had propelled her to a bad place. He didn't want to make the situation worse, but it wouldn't be right to leave her alone in the hallway.

"You know me. I'm Tony. I live right there." He pointed to his open apartment door. "Come inside before you get hurt." He reached to her and lightly clasped his hand around hers as she went to pull away.

In doing so, she almost lost her balance. He was able to pull her back upright against him. Once she was against his body, it was easy enough to gently pull her away from the mess and toward his door. She went with him as if she were in a fog.

"Is there someone I can call for you?"

He kicked his suitcase against the apartment door, forcing it completely open. He walked beside her until they were inside his apartment. He stopped beside the entrance to his living room and put the hand he'd been holding up against the wall. Leaving her, he moved across the space and grabbed his desk chair. The swivel legs fought him as he propelled it in her direction. He had to all but push the chair behind her legs to make her sit down.

When she did, she only looked with a blank stare,

the white card still crushed between her fingers. He positioned her near his hallway door to make sure she didn't feel trapped.

He left her and came back with a broom, a dustpan, and his kitchen garbage pail along with a plastic bottle of cold water. He put the cleaning supplies aside, twisted off the cap, and kneeled before her, the water an offering. She looked from him to the bottle and back several times. Then she looked at the card in her hand and closed her eyes. She didn't cry or sob.

Her fingers tightened around the paper she held. Her empty hand came up to rub her temple, and he knew she was dealing with her fear in her own way. He'd leave her alone but in full view of the hallway in case she panicked. He put the water bottle beside the chair and walked to the hallway with the supplies.

He pulled the flowers free from the pile of debris and swept as much of the glass, water, and marbles into the dustpan as he could. After several passes he figured he had most of it. He glanced around the hallway to make sure there were no marbles left as booby traps for the neighbors and waited in the doorway to his apartment until she looked at him with tear-filled eyes. He moved past her, the garbage pail in one hand and the dustpan and broom in the other. He'd left the pile of roses on the floor in the hallway.

****

Vaughn realized where she was when she heard the glass hitting the bottom of a garbage can. She was too frightened to move. When he appeared in the doorway with a broom and a pail, she held back a laugh. She was suddenly embarrassed by the whole situation. Before she could think about what she'd done or how it would look to a stranger, he was back, kneeling beside her chair.

"Would you like coffee or something stronger?" His voice was low but direct, comforting.

She finally let her gaze meet his, only to find a look of concern on his manly features. Having never been this close to him, she studied his face. His almost-too-long nose showed he hadn't been afraid of a fight, his lips were thick, and for a second time she wondered how he kissed. She'd been right about the graying hair at his temples. Today he needed a shave, and his eyes looked tired.

"Can you come inside, or do you want to stay here?"

She realized he was trying to be patient with her and shook herself from the stupor she'd allowed the gift to throw her headlong into. It had been two years since she'd felt like that. The memories had washed over her in a wave of panic like never before. "I'm sorry," she managed.

"Coffee or brandy?"

She only shook her head. She didn't want either. She wanted—no, needed—to get home and check her space. She needed to know if someone had been inside her home. Explaining it to a stranger would take forever, and she hadn't known him long enough or well enough to trust him. She tried to smile and make a joke about the whole situation.

"It's been so long since anyone sent me flowers," she began, knowing he knew she was lying. He watched her, and then it struck her—his stance, his eyes, "cops' eyes," as her dad would say.

"I find that hard to believe. Maybe you just don't

like roses," he teased and then let out a relieved breath.

She fought back the tears that filled her eyes and turned from him.

"I have coffee brewing," he said. "It should be ready. Can you come inside?"

She was behaving like a child and hated herself for it. But she had to work through this in her own time. She shook her head and closed her eyes. Her fingers crushed the card so she couldn't read the words. She knew he left her, felt the difference in the air around her, yet she was still frozen to the seat. His suitcase still held the hallway door open. She was thankful he had the forethought not to close her in.

Back beside her, he handed her a mug of steaming black coffee before dropping to the hallway floor beside her chair. He carried a similar one and was careful not to let it spill as he sat. His long legs straightened in front of him, leaving him facing her. He sipped from his cup and watched her.

She gathered her courage. "I'm sorry. I feel so silly."

"Do you want to talk about it?" he asked, his voice gentle.

"*No.*" She couldn't look at him. "It's silly. I just lost hold of the vase."

"And you scream like you're being murdered every time someone sends you flowers?" His lips curled into a little smirk, with his words leaving her no doubt he knew she was lying. She flinched when he used the word *murder*.

"I'm a klutz. What can I tell you? Always have been and probably always will be."

"All right, I can accept that for now." He pulled his

31

legs up closer to his body, leaving him sitting cross-legged beside her chair. It also left him closer.

She tried not to stare and lost the battle. "You're a cop." It wasn't a question. It was a statement of fact.

"Retired, actually. Did Gus tell you that?"

"No, it's just the look about you."

"And what makes you know the look of a policeman?" He said it with laughter, and she smiled.

"My father is…was a cop." She didn't give any more details, and he didn't ask. The way she slipped and went from "is" to "was" brought up too many questions and too many potential landmines to sort through at the moment.

"And does this cop's daughter have a name?"

She straightened in her chair. There was no avoiding it this time. "Vaughn Matthews," she managed to utter, letting her gaze linger a bit longer before turning away. He triggered inner feelings she'd put aside long ago. Now they were coming closer to her, and while she didn't fear the sexual tension building between them, it was a waste of both of their time. She didn't form relationships with men for sexual pleasure. In reality, she'd only formed friendships with men who were older and didn't trigger emotions.

He sat back from her, taking in her profile. For a long time, they were quiet. He suddenly leaned forward with acknowledgment on his face. "As in Vee Matthews from the radio?"

Her head spun around to meet his gaze too quickly, and the chair swiveled with her, sloshing coffee over the rim of the mug and onto his denim-covered leg below her. "I'm sorry. Did I burn you? See? I told you I was a klutz." She reached down to brush the liquid away but hesitated before she touched him, quickly pulling her hand back.

"No, it's fine. Are you that Ms. Matthews?"

"Yes." She couldn't lie about it. She'd made her own trap, and now she had to figure out how to gracefully get out of it.

"I've enjoyed your programing."

"Thanks, but I should be going. I have to…" No excuse came to mind.

"It's okay, Vaughn. You can leave whenever you want."

It was a statement. One that made her relax, so she sipped at the cooled coffee, watching him over the rim.

"Would you like to come inside? I could get you some fresh coffee."

"*No.*" She pulled a deep breath. "I mean…no, thanks. But thanks for your help with the flowers." She stood and handed him the half-full mug. "I'm sorry to be such a bother. I should go." She all but vaulted over his suitcase, and once in the hallway, drew in deep breaths to steady her nerves.

Chapter Three

He followed her, hesitating in his doorway. He finally walked to her as she fumbled with her keys, the card still clutched in her hand. Tony took the keyring from her trembling fingers, unlocked the door, and returned them. When she reached for them, he caught a glimpse of the writing on the card. Tactfully, he moved away while she punched in her alarm code.

When the alarm beeped, she pushed open the door. She moved inside and pressed numbers. Just before she shut the door, she apparently realized he was still standing there. Her big doe eyes questioned him. He simply held the dozen bloodred roses out to her. She shook her head, and he moved back from the door. She closed it quickly, and he heard the locks click in place.

Back in his apartment, he pulled his suitcase farther inside and locked himself in. He put the flowers under his arm and took his empty mug and her half-full one to the kitchen, where he let the roses drop onto the counter. He rinsed both cups, refilled one for himself, and then turned to stare at the flowers.

Rummaging around under his sink, he found an old clear-glass vase and filled it with fresh water. He dropped the long stems into the container, wondering where it came from in the first place, and then it struck him. He'd gotten several arrangements after he'd been shot. He never understood why he'd kept the vase and acknowledged he probably hadn't. His mother and sister had taken to coming over those first weeks and picking up around him. One of them must have rescued it. Now he was thankful they had.

He put the vase on the kitchen table and pulled out a chair. He let his weight drop heavily onto it. Then he used his feet to drag a second chair closer and unceremoniously propped his legs up on it. Staring at the red roses, he remembered the words printed on the card she'd mangled in her hand.

I found you, it read.

It set off a multitude of questions in the back of his mind. He paused to enjoy the intense feeling of recognition. He'd finally figured out where he'd heard her voice. She'd been lulling him to sleep these past weeks. But it still didn't answer the main problem at hand.

Just who else had found Vaughn Matthews, and why had it sent her into such a panic?

****

Vaughn felt stupid and childish. Overreacting like that was one of the things she'd struggled to put behind her. But when she'd read the card, the words had brought it all back—the fear, the pain, and the betrayal. She was thankful Tony had been there to help her yet regretted it at the same time. Now was not the time for developing intimate relationships with any man. Now was the time to find herself.

His kind eyes and rugged jawline didn't help. His cheeks were roughened with a five o'clock shadow, making him look tougher. She flushed at the warmth inside her and laughed out loud. It had been a long time since she'd been physical with a man, and it would be a long time before she trusted any man enough to become romantically involved, a concept that scared her almost as much as the message on the card.

Alone, she knew the rules. With a partner, she always wondered. And she had to admit she did have a lousy history of picking men.

She went through the daily homecoming ritual of checking for intruders, and finding nothing out of the ordinary, she forced herself to take a hot bath. She listened to the television all evening, staring blankly at the screen, huddled under the comforter in the center of her bed. She slept off and on and wished it were a night she was working. She was awake anyway, so why not do something useful? Yet the energy and ambition never came. At midnight, she reached for the telephone and dialed.

"Yeah." The gruff voice on the other end of the line didn't deter Vaughn.

"Yeah, yourself, you old fart." She laughed. "No wonder you have no friends. You chase them away when they call." His laughter filled the air around her, and she was instantly warm and safe again.

"And you just don't take the hint! What's up, Blondie? You okay, or do you want to come home?"

"I'm okay, and I'm not coming home. Can't a girl call her guy to say hello without him thinking she wants to run home?"

"Sure, any other time yes, but we spoke two nights ago. What's happened?"

She let out a deep breath and filled him in on her afternoon. "I got flowers with a card."

"Who were they from?" His tone sounded anxious.

"I don't know for sure. The card said, 'I found

you.' "

"Come home, Vaughn."

"No."

"I can't protect you there," he said, his voice now filled with angst.

"I'm not asking you to rescue me, just..." What did she want from him at the moment?

"Just what? Sit here and wait for some sicko to find you?"

"Just talk to me, let me vent, and tell me it will be all right."

"So you want me to start lying to you now," he answered, his tone sounding relieved.

"Yes, definitely." Her tense muscles started to relax.

"Tell me what happened."

****

"So, you see, besides overacting, I made a fool of myself with my new neighbor."

"Give me his name, and I'll check him out."

"I don't think that's necessary. The marshals told me they checked everyone in the building before I even looked at the apartment."

"Yeah, well, I'll make a few calls anyway. We'll both feel better. Vee, are you going to call the marshals and let them know about this?"

She hesitated before she spoke, her decision made. She chose her words carefully. "I don't think so. It could be someone who listens to my radio show."

"I don't like the wording."

"Neither did I, Jacob. I guess the wording was what made me panic."

"Call Daniels, just to keep him posted. And

promise me, Vee, if anything else happens, you'll let me know. I can be on a plane any time you need me."

"Thank you, Jacob. I know you'd come if I asked. But I need to be on my own, or there was no sense in leaving Seattle. Just be here for me to cry to occasionally, all right?"

"All right, but promise you'll let Daniels know."

"I will, and I'll call you next Sunday night." Hanging up, she accepted that it was cowardly to have used Jacob as a safety net, but tonight she'd needed to hear his voice. She understood that she shouldn't call her parents, so who did that leave? At least Jacob knew how to circumvent the call being traced. She'd call Daniels in the morning just for her own peace of mind.

****

Tony waited as patiently as he could while the guard checked him through the new security procedure. Since he left the force, the routine had changed drastically, and he understood the necessity. He was finally handed a guest pass and clipped it onto his jacket. He waited until a young man came to collect him and guide him to his appointed office.

Eli Griffiths glanced up as the door opened and nodded to a chair across from his desk. Thanking his guide, Tony slipped into the seat and dropped his overcoat and laptop case onto the other chair. He tried not to listen to Eli's end of the conversation, focusing instead on the new pictures standing proudly on the credenza behind the old man. They hadn't seen each other in over two years, and the years had been hard on Eli. His once-dark hair shot with gray was now gray shot with dark. The laugh lines around his lips and eyes had deepened, and he'd lost a tremendous amount of weight. Tony settled back in the seat and waited for the call to end.

"So you finally found time to come and visit me."

"And you finally found the time to invite me," Tony answered back sharply. The two held each other's look for just seconds before both of them laughed. "It's good to see you, but is it really you? The Eli Griffiths I knew was about a hundred pounds heavier and had dark, wavy hair."

"And the Tony Lombardo I knew had better sense than to taunt an old man about his appearance, especially when he was asking for a favor." Again, they eyed each other and finally laughed outright.

"How's the family? Is that a new grandbaby Darcy's holding? I missed that one."

"Everyone did," Eli answered, filling Tony in on his youngest daughter's latest escapade. "The father's back in Italy, and I doubt he'll ever be heard from again, but Darcy loves the baby, and I have to admit he's starting to win me over too."

"I'm sure all he had to do was grab his grandpa's finger once, and you were hooked for life."

Minutes later, social updates completed, Eli moved the stack of papers from in front of him. "Why are you here, Tony?"

The meeting went about how he'd expected. He got no new information, only confirmed the same that was in his files. No, Danielle Rimon-Aubin wasn't in the program, and they had no clue as to her whereabouts. He knew it would be a dead end, but he had to check anyway. It was too early for lunch, and Eli had already told him he would not be able to get away. He did, however, walk him out to the elevator.

While they said goodbye, Tony caught a glimpse of several men gathered around a receptionist's desk. The youngish woman seemed to be holding her own among the group, so he dismissed them and turned back to Eli's comments.

Outside, the air had turned cold and the sky looked as if snow was ready to fall in buckets. He took the subway home, stopping at his second favorite bar for a quick beer. One turned into three. By the time he stepped back out onto the sidewalk, a dusting of the white stuff already covered the city.

The temperature had dropped, and he decided to walk the rest of the way instead of trying to get a cab. By the time he reached his building, he was cold and tired, and worst of all, it was a completely nonproductive use of his time. The visit with Eli was personal, and the business they conducted minimal, only confirming his original thoughts.

Spending the afternoon at the bar was a waste, especially since he hated soccer and it was playing on all the screens in the dark space, yet he had enjoyed the freedom of the act itself. Never before had he been able to while away a cold afternoon on something as trivial as a soccer game.

The elevator let him out on the fourth floor, and he turned to find Vaughn Matthews in the far corner, a large hulk of a man leaning over her. He sized up the situation and didn't like it. He coughed loudly, and they split apart. He forced himself to walk calmly to his door and mutter "good evening" in their direction.

Neither Vaughn nor her male companion acknowledged him. He let himself into his apartment but hesitated before closing the door completely. He noticed the way the man entered the apartment first while Vaughn waited in the hallway. She craned her neck to see into her own home, not entering until moments later.

The whole scene left him with a strange feeling. He hung up his overcoat and forced himself to do the same with his suit jacket and pants. He dropped the tie in the drawer and grabbed a pair of sweatpants. He flipped on the television as he passed on his way to his desktop computer. It came to life with a swish and a whirl while he pulled on the sweatpants for warmth. The television news told him the snow was just beginning, and he tuned it out, still frustrated with his research being another dead end.

Hours later, lying on his bed, he listened as Vaughn Matthews told him he wasn't alone. He sat bolt upright in his bed, the vision clear in his mind. His mind sprang back to leaving Eli earlier in the day and the men gathered around the receptionist. One of them was the same man who Vaughn had brought home with her tonight. Interesting, very interesting. Was he a date, or was there a lot more to Vaughn Matthews than met the eye?

He pushed back the blanket and turned up the volume on his radio. The computer came to life with just a touch of a button and was ready for him to type in his inquiry. He went back to the bedroom for a pair of white sweat socks and pulled them on as well as his old terry cloth robe. Detouring to the kitchen, he flipped on the ever-ready coffee pot and headed back to work.

What he found disturbed him. Vaughn Matthews existed. But she existed almost a little bit too neatly. Nothing glaring or out of place. Maybe that was it? Her history was too perfect. Everyone had some transgression in their past, even a minor one. She had none. Her degrees, her credit rating all read like a perfect life. But Tony knew she hadn't had a perfect life. He'd witnessed her panic attack. He knew from experience panic like that was induced over time. Now he just had to figure out how it was induced and why. The thought that it was none of his business crossed his mind.

Something about her hit him on a gut level. Not many women got to him. The cynic inside him always found fault with them. He'd found lots of faults with Vaughn. Only somehow it made him want to know why. It didn't help that every time he thought of her, he lost control of his penis, and it stood at attention with just a passing thought of touching her.

While he never had a problem in the past, it had been a while since he'd bothered to take the time to get to know a woman. Hell, he didn't know Vaughn at all. Yet she was twisting his emotions and his hormones as if he were a sixteen-year-old kid. Something wasn't right.

It struck him there was no mention of parents in her bio. She had told him her father was a cop. That should have been in the information. Yet her bio said she was orphaned at a young age, cared for by the state. He dug deeper, trying to find any policeman killed in the line of duty during the time she was a child. None matched. There also weren't any who matched from a death off duty. Something didn't fit. He had his loose end. Did he pull the thread or walk away?

He didn't bother to go back to bed. Instead, he took his coffee to the bedroom window and watched the night turn into a dark, dank, snowy day. He dressed around six and took the subway to Brooklyn.

****

He was there in time to help his father shovel the sidewalks and stairs of their home, his sister's, and Mrs. Bonito's, who lived between them. His mother's wish was that when Mrs. B finally gave in to old age that Tony would buy her house. Then her whole family would live on the same block, a reality he tried to talk her out of each time she mentioned it.

Hours later, when he was inside and warm in his parents' kitchen, his mother put steaming bowls of vegetable soup in front of him and his father before asking what was wrong. He attempted to push off her question but only got the usual bored look from both his parents. After a couple of spoonfuls of the thick, flavorful broth, he let the spoon drop into the bowl.

"All right, but this doesn't leave this room." It was a needless request because his parents had always been the soul of discretion when he came to them with a problem.

First, he told them about his trip to Philadelphia. "George Aubin didn't seem guilty, going by my gut. I don't know why other than instinct." He told them about the second meeting with Danielle's parents. "I can understand their overwhelming grief and need to position blame, but none of it fits." He paused and ladled more of the hearty soup into his bowl. "George kept his job and the same home he lived in with Danielle. He never claimed the small insurance policy that was on her or tried to have her declared legally dead until now. He could have done it years ago."

"No boyfriends?" his father asked.

"None ever found. Now with all this time passed, George finally requested the court to declare her legally dead so he could get on with his life and remarry."

"I assume you checked on George too, to see if he had any companions?"

"None ever found. His new bride-to-be seems clean too." He shook his head. "I don't see any real resemblance to Danielle, only the brown hair. I think she left on her own."

"If she did, what was her reason?" his mother asked.

"Damned if I know," he said with a grin. "Her parents are pretty tightly wound, apparently were even before the disappearance. Gave everyone the impression they were the all-American family living the dream."

"What would you know about being a normal family?" his mother teased.

"Thank God we'll never know." He blew her a kiss across the table.

Later over coffee and almond cookies for dessert, his mother asked him what the other thing bothering him was. This time he hemmed and hawed.

"There isn't much to tell. A woman who panicked when she received red roses, who doesn't introduce herself. She obviously wanted no part of me."

"So she must be crazy," his mother said. "Who could resist this face?" She paused to drop a kiss on the top of his head before refilling their coffee cups. "So what's got you all knotted up inside?"

He sighed but continued. "Her history. It's all too clean. And she mentioned a father who was on the force, but I can't get a trace on him either."

"A person with such a clean history doesn't make sense either." His father sat back in his seat. "I'm sure you checked off-duty deaths." He shook his head. "Of course you did."

Tony wasn't going to add that he thought he recognized her date. Then he remembered why he started this conversation. "All right, the last piece of the puzzle. I caught a glimpse of a man with her last night. I'd put money on him being one of the men I saw when I visited Eli. So that puts him on a federal level, somehow. He was comfortable in the offices, not a visitor."

"Are you sure it was the same man?" Tony the Fourth asked.

"I'm ninety percent sure."

"Then you still don't have ten percent of your puzzle," his mother mused.

While he had no real answers, he did feel better by the time he got home that night.

Chapter Four

Three days later, Tony heard her familiar blood-curdling scream from the hallway. He ran to the door and saw Vaughn, standing frozen, the look of panic on her terrorized face now familiar. He glanced around and saw they were alone. He armed his alarm and pulled the door shut, not bothering with the key locks. He moved slowly toward her. There was a large, red-and-white heart-shaped box at her feet. Again, she grasped a small white card. He had no idea what it read, but this time it didn't matter. He approached her slowly and positioned himself beside her door, his back to the wall, waiting until she came out of her fog.

Just when he thought she might not, she blinked several times and fisted her hands at her sides. She fought her way back from the memory that scared her, just as she had the first time. He smiled but didn't attempt to talk or touch her. He studied the cellophane-covered box at her feet. Using a blue-and-white bandana from his back pocket, he carefully picked it up and gave it a quick once-over. He moved around her and stood it in the far corner of the hallway. When out of her sight line, he spoke.

"Vaughn?"

She looked at him and back to the card in her hand.

"I have coffee on. Would you like a cup?"

She shook her head. "No."

"How about a drink, then?" He tried a teasing tone, and she stepped back. Realizing it was the wrong approach, he pushed his hands in his back pockets—a nonthreatening move, he hoped. He leaned against the wall and waited her out. What seemed like hours was probably only two or three minutes.

Slowly she seemed to come back to the present. Her face turned red, her chin first, and then the color chased up her cheeks. She was covered from head to toe in dark wool. Only her face was visible beneath the knitted hat and the scarf pulled tight around her throat.

****

Vaughn was mortified. Twice now this stranger had seen her go to pieces. His timing was strange. She asked without hesitation, knowing her question would seem rude, not caring. "Don't you ever go out or work or something?" She held his look, studying him. She didn't expect him to burst into laughter.

"Or something," he answered. "I'm retired and work from my apartment now."

"Oh" was all she managed to get out. She had known that. Jacob had sent her an email copy of the file of information he'd collected on Tony. He even suggested he might be a good ally in the building. He was close and worked from home. He was as good a safety net as one could get without hiring a private guard. They had joked about it during their last telephone call. Her initial reaction was she didn't need a bodyguard.

"The coffee should be ready by now. Would you like a cup?" he said again.

"You must think I'm a very strange woman, Mr. Lombardo the Fifth." She'd come back to herself and the present. Thankfully, this time her panic hadn't lasted as long.

"I can only assume you don't like chocolate any better than roses." Her face paled, and he hurriedly added, "I'm sorry. That was stupid of me to say."

"No, it wasn't. You've been more than kind to me, a total stranger."

"You're not a stranger, Vaughn. You're my neighbor. I'll tell you a secret if you're ready to hear one."

Not knowing where he was going, she stood tall, preparing herself for what might come. "What?" Her tone was a little too sharp.

"Maybe now's not the time."

"Probably. I'm sorry to have interrupted you." She started to unlock her door but paused before reaching for the alarm pad.

"I'll get rid of that if you'd like." He nodded to the candy heart he'd moved earlier.

"Please. It's garbage, if you don't mind." She shivered as she glanced over her shoulder at it one last time.

Tony used his handkerchief to pick it up again. He moved away, and she called after him, her voice agitated.

"Don't eat any of it!"

This time he stopped dead in his tracks and turned to look at her. The distance didn't make his studying her any easier. "Should I have it checked for fingerprints?"

"Poison, more likely." She'd said the wrong thing again. What was it about him that had her forgetting all the training she'd put herself through? Something about his dark eyes and his day's growth of beard made him look safe. Crazy. He was a total stranger. Just because he used to be a policeman didn't make him automatically safe. She'd learned that the hard way and still carried the scars to prove it.

"I'm sorry to have bothered you again." She slid her finger over the pad, punched in her pin, and pushed the door open. "Thanks, Tony," she mumbled as she forced herself to go inside.

****

He saw her door shut and heard the locks click back in place. What would she be doing right now? He figured she'd either be going to pieces in her hallway or checking her apartment to make sure it hadn't been broken into. Either way, he knew what he was going to do.

Back in his apartment, he took the candy and placed it inside an old plastic grocery bag and then jumped in a quick shower and dressed. He still knew a few people at the lab. It was time to call in a favor.

****

A few days later, Tony hung up the telephone, the call breaking his concentration. He was never going to finish the novel he was trying to read. That was the third call in a week letting him know someone was checking on him. His old police captain had called earlier and now Eli. His bank had been the first call, asking him if he was changing his access codes. He'd made a trip down there, spoke with a vice president, and put a second safety code on all his accounts.

The fact that somebody was searching his past left him with many unanswered questions. Just who was checking him out and why? And why so blatantly? He

49

could only imagine it had something to do with the Danielle Rimon case, but who and why needed to be answered.

The knock on his door was strange. Neither doorman ever let anyone up to visit him without announcing the visitor. Even his parents and sister weren't excused from the routine.

He stopped at his desk to pull his old revolver from the drawer. He checked it quickly before he stuffed it in the back waistband of his jeans and moved to the hallway door. When he looked through the peephole, he relaxed and got an instant erection. She was appealing on a new level, something he couldn't name yet.

He wasn't sure why she was at his door holding out a cake as if it were a trophy, but he was glad she was there. A smile slipped onto his lips. This was the first time she hadn't been covered from head to toe in severe-weather gear. In a turtleneck sweater, she was much smaller and thinner than he'd originally thought.

He glanced back into his apartment to view it as she might and congratulated himself on it not being strewn with laundry. Except for stacks of books and newspapers, it was reasonably in order. His workspace was another story. The proverbial bomb had exploded there. To an outsider, it would seem a mess, but to him, it was an exercise in organized chaos.

****

Vaughn was about to leave when she heard his voice through the door.

"Hold on a minute." Then the locks clicked, and the door opened with a whoosh.

She shouldn't have attempted this personal thank-you. She was inviting trouble she didn't need. But that thought had been overridden by the need to see him again on her own terms. Just once, she wanted to be the together, new Vaughn Matthews, not the fragile, falling-apart, old Vivian whom he'd met twice. She pasted a smile on her face and held her hands forward, her offering covered in plastic wrap.

"Hello."

"Hi. I hope I'm not interrupting something important. I just wanted to…to give you this." She all but thrust the cake at him.

He didn't reach for it. Instead, he moved away from the door, pulling it open to allow her access. "Come in. I can use a break." He walked down the hallway into his living area.

She didn't care if he noticed she didn't close the door after her. She took several small steps into the now-familiar hallway, still holding the plate as far away from her as her arms would allow.

"I was just going to put on a fresh pot of coffee. Care to join me?" He disappeared into the kitchen. "What kind is it?"

"A pound cake. I wasn't sure what you'd like."

"Can you come inside, or are you afraid?"

Was he trying to push a button somewhere deep inside her? Testing her, she decided, as he reentered his living room just in time to watch her straighten her stance at the realization of his tactic. She narrowed her eyes at the reference to their past meetings and took a step farther into his home.

She glanced at the open doorway to the hall but didn't go back to close it. "I'm not afraid of you, Mr. Lombardo." Her statement was meant to reassure herself as much as him. "I just wanted to bring you this.

You've been very kind to me the last few times we've met. I figured I owed you a thank-you."

"That's very nice, and I like pound cake, but it wasn't necessary. Do you take milk or sugar in your coffee?"

He effectively worked past her escape words.

"Personally, I think sugar takes away from the taste, but a little milk just brings out the flavor." He paused and gave her a wide smile. "I'll leave the door open if you're more comfortable. Please have coffee with me."

Now she had a decision to make. First, one side of her was curious about him. He made her feel giddy, feminine for the first time in...ages. Second, she wouldn't give him the satisfaction of seeing her run again. Third, Jacob had reinforced he could be a good ally if she needed that one day. Everyone needed friends. Hell, she could fantasize anyway, as long as she kept her hands to herself.

He disappeared, and she heard movement and dishes. She stood in the same place, taking in the masculine room around her. Every space she could see was painted tan. The carpet was a darker shade, and his sofa and armchair were tan tweeds. His coffee table and side table were dark wood. No artwork hung on the walls. By his fireplace sat an old leather club chair, the seat broken in with years of use. The ottoman pulled up in front of it held a stack of newspapers and several books. The floor lamp behind the chair was turned on and so bright she thought it would blind anyone who looked directly at it.

On the seat was a pair of glasses. As she scanned the room a second time, she realized they were all over the place. Another pair was on the coffee table, another on the mantel above the fireplace. She counted two more pairs on the drafting table that was covered with paperwork. It was odd. The room was reasonably in order except for that corner. There, the wall behind was covered with pages and photos. She wanted to see what he was working on but knew not to invade his privacy.

Just when she decided to sneak a peek anyway, he pushed through the kitchen doorway carrying a wooden tray. He moved to the coffee table and nodded at her to follow him. He made small talk about the weather while putting out plates and then a fork and spoon on top of each paper napkin. He took the sugar bowl and matching creamer from the tray and put mugs beside each plate. Next came a knife. Vaughn pulled back a slight shiver. At least it was a butter knife, not a butcher knife. But even that could be deadly if wielded properly.

"Have a seat. The coffee's ready. I'll be right back." He left with the empty tray only to return with a full pot of coffee. It smelled heavenly, and she was instantly hungry.

Vaughn admonished herself. She was just going to drop off the cake, thank him for his kindness toward her, and leave. Staying to share the home-baked morsel wasn't part of her plan. If she'd thought about the possibility of sharing it with him, she wouldn't have baked for him.

He poured hot liquid into each cup. Slowly, she moved to the chair, a safe distance away from the sofa and coffee table separating them. He took a seat and nodded to the plate she still clutched. He reached forward, and she let him take it from her.

She half listened to his talk about his mother—or was it a grandmother?—who baked. It was hard to concentrate on what he was saying. She stared with wonderful thoughts of him touching her racing through her mind. Forcing herself back to the present, she accepted the slice of cake he handed her and only used a few drops of the milk in her coffee. She didn't try to eat the cake. It would stick in her throat. Rather she chose to sip the coffee, watching him over the rim of the mug.

"Good cake, moist and buttery. Do you cook for yourself often?"

"It comes in waves. It soothes me to bake. I find it very satisfying, as long as I have somebody to share the result with. Otherwise, I'd be four hundred pounds by now."

"Well, from now on feel free to bake away. I'll accept any of your leftovers."

He smiled when he said it, and she relaxed into the comfortable tan chair. They danced verbally around the cold weather for a while, and it wasn't until he paused to refill both their cups that the quiet between them became intense.

"There was no poison in the candy." He took his mug and pushed back on the sofa.

Her gaze flew to his face, but she didn't dare speak.

"There were several sets of fingerprints, but none of them were identifiable. That doesn't mean much. They're probably from the production process and store handling. Whoever left it for you didn't want you to be able to identify them." He watched her closely as she tried to act nonchalant.

"I thought you were teasing about the fingerprints. I figured you'd just toss it down the incinerator."

"Do you really not like chocolate, or have you been taught never to trust something if you don't know where it came from?"

He hit too close to home, and she squirmed in her chair. She lifted the mug to her lips to hide from his inspecting look.

"I checked with Gus. Both the flowers and candy were delivered by different people. The flowers by a woman he knows from the local florist, and the candy by a bicycle messenger." He viewed her over his mug as he drank. "I checked with the florist. They were paid for in cash, but the clerk doesn't remember the customer. Unfortunately, they didn't catch any good views of him on their surveillance cameras. I haven't been able to trace the candy."

"Why?"

"Why haven't I been able to trace it, or why did I do it at all?"

"Yes." She laughed nervously and reached forward to pull a small corner of her slice of cake from the larger piece on her plate. She ate several morsels before looking back at him.

"Habit mostly. Once a cop, always a cop."

She nodded. "Did Gus think you were crazy or just me?"

"Neither. Gus walked a beat for twenty-five years. He took this job because being at home with his wife drove them both crazy. I knew him from my rookie days on the force."

"I suppose I should feel better knowing you're across the hall and Gus is downstairs. Funny, my original information didn't tell me about Gus."

"But you do feel better. Don't you, Vaughn? Is it a stalker who's got you tied up in knots?"

"It's nobody. Just old...old habits die hard sometimes." She took the paper napkin and wiped her fingers, refusing to look at him. "You make good coffee. What brand do you use? Mine always tastes like cardboard."

"Are you being stalked, Vaughn?"

This time he had her attention. She closed her eyes and let out a deep sigh. Leaning forward, she put the mug down and folded her hands in her lap.

"Or are you running away from someone? A husband, boyfriend, or lover?" Again, he waited her out; only this time he leaned forward, his hand on his knee.

The position brought him closer, closer than she was comfortable with. She took the defensive. "What makes you think I'm being stalked or that I've run away from a husband?" She tried to laugh away his question, but it wasn't working. She let her gaze stray around the room and land on the photographs tacked over his desk. "I thought you said you were retired from the force?" He accepted her avoidance and didn't verbally challenge her. "Do you always answer your door armed?" She let herself have a laugh at besting him. She'd seen his gun tucked in his waistband.

His smile warmed her. Knowing the effect he could have on her, she made up her mind this would be her first and last visit. Jacob said he had a good reputation and was basically an all-around nice guy, just what she didn't need. She'd finish her coffee and never come back.

"I'm retired. I'm investigating an old case, just making sure nothing was missed."

"A cold case kind of thing? Can you discuss it, or is it confidential? What?" she said, acknowledging his surprised look. "I watch television with all those documentaries about police and their work."

He watched her carefully for a few minutes, apparently deciding what to do. He rose and walked to the desk, put his gun on top, and took down a photograph from the wall.

The woman was pretty and had dark hair and dark eyes. She had a kind smile. It looked like a graduation picture from the black sweater she wore and the thin circle of pearls that wound around her throat.

Vaughn didn't know if it was a high school or college photo. Judging by the hairstyle, it must have been twenty years old. "She's very pretty. Who is she?" She held the photo, looking at it from all angles.

"Her name is…was…is," he corrected, "Danielle Rimon-Aubin. She disappeared many years ago, without a trace."

"How awful for her family."

"Yes, it is. They've asked me to investigate her disappearance."

"From the look of your desk, you're not having any luck, are you?" Her lips curled into a smile. "Want to talk about it?"

"Do you?"

Her interest surprised him. He probably thought she was trying to divert attention from herself. The question would keep her with him a little bit longer, a few minutes to memorize his face.

"Why now? Why wait all this time?"

"There wasn't much anyone could do. At the time all the possibilities were exhausted." He watched as she propped the photo on the table and looked at it from a distance. "Her parents contacted me a few months ago when they heard her husband wanted to get remarried. To do that he had to petition the courts to declare her legally dead. That didn't sit well with them, to say the least. He could have done it years ago but chose not to."

"The husband, aren't they always the first suspect and then the family?" She knew a lot about missing people, but she didn't explain how, except to say "I used to watch a lot of television shows."

"Yes, they checked him and her family at the time. All came up clean. The husband had a clean alibi, a teacher who never left the building all day, coached a basketball game that evening. Hell, there were more people willing to testify he'd been where he was supposed to. They even had home videos of him at the practice and the game. He reported her missing when she didn't come home that evening. He made calls to friends and family, called the hospitals and then the police."

"And I assume her family checked out?"

"Yeah, both accounted for, with no changes in pattern. Danielle simply left her job one afternoon and was never heard from again. They never found her car either."

"I assume bank accounts were monitored?" Vaughn leaned closer to the photo again, as if she might see something everyone else has missed.

"All accounted for. The husband didn't claim the small life insurance policy, and he almost went bankrupt paying for private investigators."

"And now he wants to get married again. Is she someone he knew while Danielle was still with him?"

"No, a new teacher in the school. She started teaching there two years ago. From what I can come up with, they were friends for a while before things went romantic. Besides, she is so many years younger they wouldn't have crossed paths. She's also from the West Coast. She only came east when she got the teaching position."

"Do you have any other pictures of her? Candid maybe?"

Tony didn't question her. He went back to the file and pulled out several other shots of Danielle, some alone and some with friends and family. On the back of each, the location, the date, and the other people were clearly marked. She looked at each one, studying them carefully. He added there was never any indication of drug use or gambling and they never found any links to a boyfriend.

"Why do men always assume it has to be a boyfriend? Did any female friends go missing around the same time?"

He sat forward, staring at her for several minutes. "No, none that I could find. I was out there recently, and everything checked out."

"Maybe she just wanted to leave for her own reasons. Is that where you were when we met?"

"Yes, I'd just come back from Philadelphia."

"Seems to me it's all so neat, no loose ends, almost too perfect."

There was a prolonged silence between them; neither flinched. "Just like you, Vaughn Matthews. All so neat, never a parking ticket or a minor arrest, never a bounced check, perfect grades."

She stood quickly, the movement making the photograph slide off the table with the current of air that moved with her. "You had me checked out? How dare you. You had no right to dig into my past."

She rushed to the door, but he was there, just behind her. When she reached her apartment, she had to pause to unlock the door. She breathed deeply, and she knew he saw the anger in her face and movements. Even her hard glare didn't make him shy away.

Waiting until she was about to punch in her code, he cleared his throat to get her attention. "Yes, I did, Vaughn. Or whatever your real name is. I didn't go too deep and set off any red flags. But a woman who freezes in fear when she gets flowers and candy tends to make a person wonder, especially if the person is a retired New York police detective. Your history is perfect, too perfect. Want to share why?"

"Maybe I've led a clean life. Is that so impossible?" She fought to gain control of her emotions and the hate in her voice.

"Technically, yes," he all but hollered back.

Tense didn't begin to describe how he made her feel. He closed the few steps between them and pulled her to him, his hands on her shoulders directing her to his body. His lips crushed hers.

She started to push him away, then relented when he softened the kiss. Her sigh gave him entry into her mouth, and his tongue flicked over hers.

She allowed him to kiss her and wound her hands up and around his neck as her fingers rested in his hair. He was the one to break contact. He stared down at her before pulling her closer. She didn't back away, didn't speak, simply rested her cheek against his shoulder.

The elevator chimed in the background, and she finally pulled away. She didn't look at him or down the hall. She angled her body to block her keypad and let herself into her apartment.

Chapter Five

Vaughn was angry with Tony and herself. How dare he check her out, she'd asked several times to nobody but herself. How dare he kiss her! That was the crux of the problem. She'd wanted him to kiss her and had done nothing to stop him. Worst of all, she wanted him, all of him. She wanted the maleness of him, his scent and his taste. She wanted to know how he'd touch her and the places he'd take her body to in the dark of the night. It had been a long time, too long, since she allowed a man to touch her. Tony made her mind work in ways that had been shut down. The concept was both exciting and daunting. The sexual thrill weighed heavily against her instinct to remain alone.

As she dressed for work, she decided it was time to shop. Maybe if she bought herself some new toys, the thought of Tony's toy wouldn't keep her awake. When he held her against him, she'd felt his erection. When he pressed against her, her intuition told her he'd be a lover like no other she had experienced.

She'd only slept with two men in the past, and neither was experienced. Ultimately, she knew his maturity would take her to a different place, a more languid plane than the groping she'd known. In her mind, Tony would love her, not just have sex with her. The idea made her smile, and that made her mad all over again. It was a vicious cycle.

Only a small hint of guilt slipped through when she remembered she'd dug into his private life too. Jacob had done some investigating. So what right did she have to be angry with him? The whole situation was out of control, and the one thing Vaughn Matthews was sure of was she wanted control over the rest of her life.

****

The knock on her door made her heart skip a beat. Tuesday, she was looking forward to a quiet night at home. The wind howled outside from arctic winds that were dropping from Canada with a cold front. No snow was predicted, only chafing wind and cold. Patrick hadn't announced anyone, and she was instantly on alert. Checking the peephole in her door, she wiped her sweat-laden palms on the thighs of her jeans before letting out a relieved breath.

It didn't help that Tony Lombardo looked good enough to eat. His dark hair still looked as if it needed a trim, but he'd shaved sometime recently. His profile was clean of any stubble. He wore an old NYPD sweatshirt and, she assumed, jeans. She took a cleansing breath before working the security system on her front door and made a conscious decision to remove the chain.

The small, oval mirror that hung just inside her doorway told her she was about as put together as she would get with no notice. Pulling the door open, she tried to smile. If only his smile didn't reach inside her to the core and wrap itself around her.

"Hi." She tried to sound unaffected by his surprise visit.

"Is this a bad time?"

She was thankful he didn't make a move to enter.

"No, not really." She wanted to offer the words to invite him in, but she couldn't form them. She stepped back and opened the heavy door wider for him to enter. It was a strange feeling, letting this man into her private space. She wondered what he would think but pushed it to the back of her mind. It was her world. She didn't begrudge him his space decorated all in beige.

He took two steps forward and refrained from cringing, she decided, as he was bombarded by the orange glow on the walls of her hallway. He extended the plate he was holding toward her, and she accepted it reluctantly, not wanting him to leave and not having the courage to invite him in. The long, silent pause between them allowed them to look each other over.

"I figured it might belong to a set." He nodded to the plate she now clutched to her chest. "I was going to ask if you wanted to grab a bite to eat, but it smells like you're already ahead of me in that department."

She was on her home ground. She shouldn't be nervous. "Beef burgundy. It was a comfort-food kind of day."

"Just like my house growing up, but it was usually the smell of tomato sauce and meatballs I came home from school to."

"Where did you go to school?" She leaned against the wall, not forcing him back to the hallway but not allowing him farther into her space. If he'd realized anything about her, it was not to push.

"Brooklyn. Didn't my accent give me away? My parents are still there." He leaned his long body against the doorframe, and his hands slipped into the back pockets of his jeans, a nonthreatening position. "My sister and her family live two doors down. It's great for both of them. My parents get to be active grandparents, and it gives Carmen a break."

"Do you see them often?"

"A lot more now that I'm off the force. My time is my own now, and the kids are at a good age for venting to someone who isn't their immediate parent figure."

"You seem to know a lot about kids. Do you have any of your own?"

"No, never married, no kids."

"Seems a shame…" She was getting way too personal. It was time to change the subject. "It's cold out tonight," she all but stammered, remembering how he pulled her against him, his body tight to hers. His kiss had started out demanding, then turned into a slow stroking of an inner flame she didn't know existed. The look on his face changed, and she realized she was talking about the weather while he was watching her with a strange look in his eye.

"The fed—is he a boyfriend or a bodyguard?"

His question was so out of left field she was taken aback. Not knowing how he knew about Daniels, she stared at him.

When he realized she was floored by his observation, he went on. "It's just that I don't tread on another man's territory."

"What makes you think he's a fed?"

She moved slowly toward the living room. Tony questioned her with his look before following. She nodded and waited for him to catch up with her after gently closing her front door.

From the archway, he lingered, admiring her home. She stood several feet away from him in the entrance to the living room and tried to see it from his perspective.

65

The walls, like the hallway, glowed a bright orange color, glossy and warm. The flames from the fireplace danced against the far wall in the darkening afternoon light.

"That's the music from *Camelot*." He recognized the soundtrack to the musical that played softly in the background.

"You know it?"

"Grew up listening to these musicals." His lips curled up into a smile as he surveyed her apartment. "That's probably why I'm drawn to your radio station."

All she could say was "Oh."

A lounge chair by the fireplace complemented a soft-looking floral couch, and the matching plaid chairs were a mix of blue, yellow, and apricot. The coffee table was light oak, as was the rest of the furniture in the room. All the trim stood out in a bold, bright, glossy white.

Throw pillows and knitted blankets added more color to the already bright sofa and chairs. The french doors to her bedroom were open, and he didn't hedge his look into her blue-green bedroom.

"Seen enough or would you like the tour?" she teased. "I know it's bright and bold, and before you ask, no, I haven't woken up with a hangover in here yet." She didn't feel threatened by him and relaxed enough to leave him standing there while she went into the kitchen.

As the door swung open and then closed, the heavenly scent wafted through the space. She returned empty-handed and stalled in the doorway. "Would you like a glass of wine? I have a hearty burgundy I opened for the stew."

"What about the fed boyfriend or guard?"

Vaughn mulled over how to answer him and took the offensive. "What makes you think he's a federal agent?" Her hands warmed her arms as she watched him. He hadn't made himself at home in her space, rather stayed where she left him.

"Same thing that made you think I was a cop—the look, the haircut, the attitude."

He gave her a crooked grin, and she wanted to drop to her knees in front of him. She smiled at the ridiculousness of the idea.

His lips curled into a smile. "I was at the federal office and saw him at a distance. Days later he's here checking your apartment before letting you go in." He ended his statement with one eyebrow raised.

Lying to him was a challenge, one she didn't take lightly.

"He's a friend, not a boyfriend. At this time in my life, I need to figure out who I am before I decide to be something to another person."

"I can accept that. Can you accept my offer of supper, or am I pushing too fast?" He let his weight slide to his other hip.

She liked that he seemed to understand her need for control and didn't question it. "How about sharing my stew?" As soon as she spoke the words, panic swelled in her belly. "I'm a fair cook, haven't killed anybody yet with my meals."

"All right, I'd like that, but only if you agree to come out with me one night as a payback."

She didn't answer but didn't turn away either. "Make yourself at home. I'll get us a glass of wine. Supper will be ready in an hour."

****

It was interesting to watch a man in her space. In her mind, Daniels didn't really count. While he had given her several outright offers of companionship or more, she'd backed away from his attempts. Mixing with him just didn't sit right. She understood his lifestyle and couldn't be involved with someone who never knew where he'd be the next day.

Tony wandered to the sofa and sat. He leaned forward and pulled one of the art history books from the pile on the coffee table. Vaughn disappeared into the kitchen and returned with two half-filled glasses. The wine was a deep-red color. After handing one to Tony, she circumvented the seating area and locked the hall door.

"So what shall we talk about that won't make you antsy?" He took a small sip of the wine.

"You talk about me as if I'm a prickly pear," she said with a smile.

"Let's just say I'm trying to stay on neutral ground." He tipped his glass toward her before taking a second sip.

He used the wine as a natural subject change, and that led to an in-depth discussion of their tastes in alcohol and wine. That particular line of conversation took them through the hour until it was time to start the rest of their meal. He offered to help her in the kitchen, and she thought to say no.

Instead, she asked him if he would mind setting the table. He was out of his seat before she finished her question. She salted a large pot of boiling water while he set the table with minimal direction. She kept busy chopping herbs and dumping them into the bottom of a large bowl, along with chunks of real butter. He took a seat, diplomatically keeping his distance, which she appreciated. The simmering beef smelled even better in the kitchen.

Tony asked her where she learned to cook and with some hesitation, she told him, "I had a lot of time on my hands at one point, and cooking was one of the few talents I was able to explore." She went no further, and he didn't push.

When the noodles were soft from their boiling bath, she dumped the strained pot on top of the butter and herbs in the bowl. Gently, she mixed the contents until the noodles were coated with the mixture. Spooning some into the bottom of each of the two deep bowls set beside the stove, she added large ladlefuls of beef and vegetables, then added gravy to the top of each. After she placed the bowls on the table, she retreated to grab the bread she had warming in the oven. Their first few mouthfuls were quiet, as she appreciated the meld of flavors of the wine and mushrooms, the onions and beef, all slowly cooked together. His compliments seemed genuine, and her lips spread into a smile of pride she'd so rarely felt.

"What can you tell me—no, what are you comfortable telling me about the time you…learned to cook? From the taste of this, you had plenty of time." He continued eating, not hesitating to sop up the rich wine gravy with the warm buttered bread.

"I can't tell you anything." She focused on her bowl. At first, she thought his question would take away her appetite, but she was still hungry and enjoying the meal she'd so lovingly created.

"That *his* orders or someone else's?"

"I've only known Daniels since I came to New York. A friend of a friend, someone to call if I...get lonely in the big city." She didn't need to look up to know he understood her avoidance.

"Vaughn, are you hiding in plain sight?"

Her head snapped up, and he motioned to the pot on the stove. She acknowledged his request with a nod but allowed him to serve himself a second helping. When he settled across from her again, he changed the subject.

"I'll tell you something if you don't hold it against me." He didn't wait for her answer. "I saw some of the debris coming out of here before you moved in and wondered what you were doing with the blue-and-yellow tile. I couldn't picture it, but somehow you made it all work. It's a very comfortable place to be. You must enjoy spending time in here."

She only nodded and pushed another forkful of beef into her mouth before she said the wrong thing.

"I'd never have imagined two colors would work together so well."

"They're buttercup yellow and teal blue, and yes, the contractor did question me several times about my choices. But I spent a lot of time in other people's spaces, most of them Spartan or dull. Here, I wanted color, as you guessed from seeing the rest of the place."

"What color did you make your bathroom?"

"White, all pristine, pure white. I change the color with accessories when I get bored." She hesitated and then added, "I suppose yours is beige?" She didn't hold back the laughter that bubbled up with her question.

"As you've noticed, I'm not much of a decorator. The apartment had just been repainted when I saw it, and I just wanted to get moved in and settled. My last place was being sold as condos, and I didn't want to buy there. I spent too much time being picky about where I was going to move, so I didn't have a lot of time to change it. Once my stuff was here and put away, I didn't have the heart to repack and start from scratch."

"Sounds logical. I've spent so much time…" She dropped her thought and changed the subject before she revealed too much about her past. "Would you like seconds?"

"I've already had seconds, but thanks, it was delicious, almost like being back in Brooklyn." He took their empty bowls to the sink and rinsed them before loading the dishwasher.

"You don't have to do that."

"I ate, I help clean, house rules growing up. Hard to break the habit. How about you pack up the leftovers while I start the pots?"

"You wash, and I'll dry. I know where the pots go." She slipped away and changed the music to an oldies radio station. They worked side by side in her new kitchen, humming to the Beach Boys and Bob Dylan. It was a good entry into her radio programming, and the conversation gave her insight into his personality.

"I was a Doors, Zeppelin, and The Who kind of kid growing up. I drove my poor folks crazy." She smiled but didn't share the memory. "I was stuck in the nineteen seventies with music. At least I wasn't blaring the current hip hop that was popular with my friends. They all thought I was a bit strange with my choices, but my parents played seventies music all the time.

They even brought me to see The Who in Dallas. It was a great concert. I was young, but I remember the music and theatrics of the concert thrilled me." She paused. Did he catch her slip regarding her parents?

He took the towel from her hands and dried his before leading her back to the table. When they were both seated, he watched her intently before speaking, as if he were choosing his words carefully. "All right, I don't have to know your past, only if you're in trouble now."

She shook her head.

"So you're not running from the police, or you wouldn't be inviting the feds in when a problem arises. I can only assume you're in the program." Tony held up his hand as if to ward off her reaction. "I don't need to know just yet. When you're ready, you'll tell me."

She only stared at him.

"In the meantime, can we continue with getting to know each other, or do you see me as a threat too?" he asked.

She rose and made a production of cleaning the sink. When the stainless steel was spot free, she turned, her arms crossed over her chest. "I can't give you details, only that I've never been in trouble with the law directly. As to our relationship, I don't know the answer. You make me nervous in a way I haven't felt in years, but I'm afraid. It's been a long time since I was on my own, and I wouldn't want to put you in any uncomfortable positions."

"Did you have your friends check me out, Vaughn? I need to know. If it wasn't you, somebody else has been checking into my private life. If it has something to do with the cold case I'm working on, I need to know. It would mean I'm getting close and somebody is getting nervous."

"A friend checked to make sure you were who you said you were. I didn't think you would find out. I'm sorry. It's rude, I understand. I know how you feel. When you mentioned you checked me out…"

"But that's because you didn't want me sending any red flags if somebody else is looking for you." He paused while she nodded. "All right, how about we just start with friends for a while and see how that goes? But you should know I want more from you. I want you in my life as a love interest with all the good and bad that comes with it. Can you handle that down the road?"

"I don't know. To be honest, I'm not sure who to trust anymore, and my judgment in the past hasn't been great. I've got the scars to prove it." Her hand went to the white cotton turtleneck covering her throat and tugged it higher.

"Jesus, who hurt you, Vaughn?"

Before she could register his move, he was out of his seat and had his arms wrapped around her, pulling her close. It wasn't a sexual move. It was a comforting hug.

"It doesn't matter anymore. It's over. Can we leave it at that? If we can't, then I don't see our friendship going any further." She chanced to look up and study his expression. He didn't turn away.

"I don't see any other choice. Someday when you're ready to tell me, I'll listen. Until then, if I get too nosy, I'm sure you'll let me know." He smiled and touched his lips to hers.

She drank in his warmth, her arms sliding up

around his neck. It was Tony who took a step back. A warm blush crept up her cheeks, and she turned back to the sink. "Coffee?"

He laughed aloud at her change of subject. "For now, coffee."

He stayed close behind as she pulled a filter from a plastic bag over the stove and counted ten scoops into the filter. She went to put in the eleventh, and he stopped her hand, laughing. She wanted to be mad, but the light in his eyes had her laughing too.

"What?"

"No wonder you say your coffee tastes like cardboard." He removed the filter from its plastic holder and dumped the coffee back in the canister. She moved aside and watched as he started again after checking the size of her pot.

"Six spoonfuls for a pot this size! You trying to keep the coffee brokers in the black?"

"My mother used to say one spoon for each cup and one for the pot."

"And did she make mud too?" he asked with a laugh. When she didn't answer, he went on. "I bet she used an old-fashioned percolator, not a drip pot."

"All right. Don't get smug on me. The guys used to tell me I was trying to kill them with my brew." She didn't acknowledge her slip referring to her past protectors. If he asked, she'd change the subject.

She moved to put hot water in the glass pot. He shook his head and took it carefully from her hands. "Cold water is best or at least room temperature, never hot water."

"Show off. This better taste as good as you make it sound, or you'll never live it down."

"Don't I know it," he quipped.

His low laughter reminded her of home, warm and comforting. He was sexy as hell in an offhand sensual way as he placed a quick kiss on her lips before asking which cabinet the mugs were in.

"That was an effective way of changing the subject," she told him, not annoyed, just letting him know she was getting his number. "Do it again, Tony."

He glanced at her, his expression revealing his surprise at her suggestion, but finished pouring the water into the back of the machine. He placed the glass pot on the warmer and flipped the On switch. Then he pulled her into his arms and kissed her the way she wanted him to, full out with no restraint.

Vaughn didn't hold back. She took what he offered and pushed for more. When his erection pressed against her belly, she let her hand slip down between their bodies, exploring the length and girth of him through the soft denim. His moan against her mouth told her she was doing something right. It wasn't until the smell of brewed coffee infiltrated their moment that she finally pulled away.

"Coffee's ready." She laid her head against his shoulder.

"So am I," he whispered, and she knew he didn't mean coffee.

She forced herself to move from his embrace to fill the cups. She offered him milk and put a few drops in her cup. With her head, she motioned for them to go back to the living room. She followed him, thankful for the fresh air and the space between them. He dropped down on the sofa, and she sat in her chair, her legs tucked up under her.

"I suppose we should talk about our pasts," he said. "I've been tested regularly, and it's been a long time since I've been in any kind of relationship that led to sex."

"I was tested for everything in the hospital, and I've been alone too. Not too many men would want me the way I looked after..." She didn't finish, and he didn't ask.

He moved to the table in front of her, then sat at eye level. "I don't care about the past, Vaughn. When you're ready, I'll listen. For now, let's just see what happens between us."

"Thank you for not pushing."

"It's in my best interest not to."

"I'm not protected. There's been no reason, and I don't need a pregnancy at this time in my life to complicate things. I need to be very careful, Tony. I'd like children someday if it's meant to be, but this isn't the right time in my life. Can you understand and accept that?"

He moved back to the sofa. "Loud and clear, Vaughn. When we're together, we'll be careful. I promise."

"Pretty sure of yourself, aren't you?"

"Sure of us both. We just need to give you some time to accept it." He rose and headed for the door. "I'm leaving now before I do something stupid and make you change your mind about me. Thanks for supper. Will you come out with me tomorrow night?"

"Not tomorrow. How about Thursday before I go to work?" She walked calmly toward him. He couldn't get out of her apartment until she let him out.

"Thursday works for me. What time?"

"Seven all right with you? It will give us time for a leisurely supper and still leave me time to come home and get ready for work."

"I'll pick you up at seven. Chinese okay?"

"Sounds wonderful. My time was up before I got into oriental cooking." She waited for his reaction, but all she got was a nod and the feeling he was holding back a smile.

"Night, Vaughn. I suppose I don't have to tell you to lock up after me?"

"That you don't. Night, Tony." As usual, she blocked the keypad with her body before opening the door.

He hesitated only for a moment before dropping a light kiss on her lips. He was gone from her space, his scent lingering in the small hallway. As she had done after meeting him the first time, she locked the door and stood several moments, waiting for her breath to return to normal. This time it wasn't from shock or fear. The warm, cozy feeling inside her made her hug her arms to her body.

She was horny, and it was about time. Too much of her time had elapsed beyond her control. With Tony, she wanted to relinquish control.

Chapter Six

Life was good for Tony. Vaughn made it that way. She seemed to be relaxing around him. Their supper turned into afternoon getaways to movies and museums. He enjoyed the luxury of not living on a predetermined schedule. While Vaughn worked nights and slept all morning, the timing allowed them the afternoons and evenings together. His work seemed to fit in around his new schedule.

He was sleeping better but only on the nights Vaughn lulled him to sleep with her voice and her music choices. He was also learning her moods. Her playlist was directly in tune with her feelings. When she was blue or melancholy, so were her choices. When she was happy, her choices were lighter. Some days she was depressed but wouldn't confide why. Most times he didn't push.

She saw him several times a week when their schedules allowed. Between his lectures at the police academy and her occasional voice-over work, they were both busy but not crazed. Their calendars allowed them the luxury of time to get to know each other.

She was so bright and alive sometimes, and at other times so dark. He'd yet to figure out the pattern. They'd become close physically, touching and kissing often, but still hadn't progressed to full-out lovemaking. On Valentine's Day, he took her to an early supper but didn't give her roses or chocolate. He'd found an old recording of Duke Ellington on vinyl in an unopened package. She'd surprised him with a book on the history of Brooklyn. He was stunned she'd gone to so much trouble. They touched easily and often, and most nights she seemed more frustrated when they parted.

****

For the first time in her adult life that she could remember, Vaughn was happy. With her work, her home, and her love life. In the depths of a cold March afternoon, she shopped for lacy undies. She chose a pale pink bra-and-panty set; she didn't want red or black just yet. She was slowly readying herself for the release of passion she'd stored up all these years. She hoped Tony would be able to release the hidden erotic side she'd never been comfortable exploring.

He never pushed her, yet he was as physical as she'd let him. He had a sixth sense about her, when she wanted him close and when to give her space. Sometimes he knew before she did what was on her mind. A few times in the last two weeks, they necked and touched like teenagers.

Each time he was the one to pull back, allowing her a graceful retreat. Whether hormones or just the cycle of the moon, she knew the timing was right. If she was ever going to trust him, it was now or never.

Without telling him, she started on the birth control pills she'd gotten from her new doctor. With a month behind her now and his promise to use protection, she figured she was as babyproof as she would ever get and still be active. Her contract with the radio station had been extended another three months, which gave her added financial security.

Her real birthday had just passed with nobody but her parents knowing. Thirty-two seemed like a milestone. The plain fact she'd survived this long was a credit to the marshals. Vaughn Matthews had chosen the day she left the protective custody of the federal marshals as her birthdate. She had months to go to make that celebration, but her future looked bright. Tony had hinted about taking her to Brooklyn to meet his family, and she was warming to the idea.

They had plans for supper and a late movie after his lecture. They'd been friends for over three months now, and she was ready to implement some of the fantasies she'd been having about him. It had been a long time since she allowed herself to care for a man, and mistake or not, she would find out if her feelings were genuine or just lust. She glanced around the apartment but didn't rush to check her traps. She put the wine in the refrigerator to chill, selected several discs for background music, and went to take a long bath.

With time to spare, she did all the little beauty routines she'd let slip these last months. Her smooth legs felt good to her hand as she renewed her promise to keep shaving even if things didn't work out with Tony.

With freshly washed hair, she checked the manicure and pedicure she'd splurged on earlier in the day. She dressed with care, watching her figure move in the new pink underwear set before pulling on clean jeans and for once, a man-tailored, button-down white shirt. She tied a gold-patterned scarf around her throat, tucking the ends inside. Satisfied her scars were covered yet in something other than her standard turtleneck, she dried her hair and used minimal makeup.

As an afterthought, she fluffed the pillows on the sofa and aligned the books on her coffee table when she saw the flashing light on her voicemail. The message must have come in while she was in the bath. She hit the Play button, smiling as she listened to Jacob's voice boom into the space.

"Hello, Blondie. I'm back from my fishing trip, just checking in. Call me Sunday or before if you need me. I hope you don't need me."

She paused in the kitchen doorway, a wineglass in each hand as the second message played. The tone of the voice made her drop the glasses.

"You know I've found you and you can't get away from me. I'm waiting to come to you…Vivian. I'll know when the time is right. Wait for me, Vaughn Matthews. I'm closer than you think."

The message ended, and she stood frozen. Doing the first thing that came to mind, she called Daniels, trying to keep the panic from her voice. "It was just a message. I don't know that you need to come by." She knew he would anyway and was thankful. She forced herself to listen to it again and couldn't place the voice.

Twice, she thought about calling Tony and dismissed it each time. She paced the apartment for the twenty minutes it took for Daniels to arrive. He pounded on the door to announce his arrival. After she opened it, she walked to the sofa and sat on the edge. She pointed to her cell phone and tried not to listen to the voice.

When it finished, she knew he was on his cell phone and didn't care who he was calling. She just wanted it to stop.

****

Tony rushed home to shower before his supper with Vaughn. He'd had the feeling she was getting close to finally trusting him, and he didn't want to blow it now. With his hair still damp, he knocked on her front door, expecting Vaughn, not Daniels, to open it.

"What are you doing here?" Tony asked without hesitation.

He and Daniels sized each other up. Daniels was about his height, but for all of Tony's darkness, Daniels was fair and blond with light blue eyes. He wasn't wearing his jacket, and his gun was holstered on his hip.

"This isn't a good time." Daniels widened his stance in the doorway, blocking Tony from entering.

"I don't care." Tony all but pushed him aside. "Vaughn." He moved quickly through the small hallway, Daniels close behind him. "Vaughn." He found her sitting in her favorite chair beside the fire. She stared into the flames, not acknowledging his presence.

He inched beside her and sat on the edge of her lounge chair. Waiting until she looked, he reached a hand out to her. She slid into his arms without question, her arms around his neck, holding on as if he'd rescued her from some horrible dream.

Tony caught the look of disgust on Daniels's face just before he turned away, his cell phone in hand. He didn't ask questions. He just held her. When she finally pulled back, he used the pads of his thumbs to wipe away the few stray tears that rolled down her cheeks.

"You're all right. Just tell me what happened." Glancing around her apartment, he saw the broken glass but didn't ask what happened.

"I just overreacted," she started.

Daniels came to attention. "No, you didn't." He pushed a button on his cell phone, and all three of them listened to the two messages on the speaker.

Tony wondered why his brunette goddess was being called Blondie but filed it away for a later date.

The second message sent instant hate through him. Vaughn tensed against him as the man's words rang through the quiet space.

When the message ended, Daniels stared at Tony. "So where were you this afternoon?"

"Stop it. We know it's not Tony," Vaughn snapped.

"You don't know anything for sure at this point."

Tony stood to his full height. He hoped the look in his eyes threatened the marshal to take his statement further. "We don't know where you were this afternoon either. Maybe you don't like the fact that Vaughn and I have formed a relationship. Maybe you don't like to think of her in my arms and not yours." His voice dripped with anger.

"Listen, you pompous little..." Daniels started.

"Just watch what names you throw around. I saw you cornering that secretary in the office a while back. You didn't manage to intimidate her, and you don't intimidate me."

"What the hell were you doing at headquarters?" Daniels asked with a confused look on his face.

"That doesn't matter. What does matter is what I saw and what we need to do about keeping Vaughn safe." His stare was equally as menacing as Daniels's.

Vaughn listened to them spar another few rounds before standing. She didn't scream, but her loud tone got both their attentions.

"Stop it, both of you. I have enough problems without you two measuring your cocks with words. Just stop it!" She looked at Tony, then Daniels and back to Tony. She left them to work it out, heading to her bathroom.

Tony wanted the confrontation with Daniels, but her apartment wasn't the place, and this wasn't the time to go a few rounds over her. He stepped away and moved into her kitchen, taking a few moments to control his temper and emotions. He returned with a broom and dustpan. He swept up the broken glass to keep busy. When he finished, he allowed himself a few minutes to regroup and figure out what Vaughn needed most.

He put on a pot of coffee and carried three mugs to the coffee table. On his second trip, he brought back the container of milk from her refrigerator. Daniels would get only this for a peace offering. Tony hoped he'd accept it, because the idea of beating his pretty face was first on his list right about now. It wouldn't help Vaughn, so he shelved it, but it would have helped him. As they stared at each other, he refrained from another verbal onslaught.

"Is this the first time he's found her by phone?" Daniels asked, his voice tight, as if each word hurt to say aloud.

"As far as I know."

"I suppose you could have altered your voice…but probably not." Daniels's tone sounded resigned to Tony's presence.

"I don't know what to think about you," Tony told him outright.

Daniels laughed openly, and it broke the tension. They sat across from each other, both with their hands folded on their laps. That was how Vaughn found them minutes later when she returned. Her hair was damp around the edges, and what little makeup she'd worn had been washed away.

She looked young and vulnerable, even though he knew she was past thirty. He wanted to protect her, to take her away from whatever this menace was doing to her. He also knew he couldn't.

"Are you two finished jockeying for position?" she asked.

From the look on her face, she was not expecting an answer. She detoured into the kitchen and returned with the full pot of coffee. Her hand shook as she poured it, so she set it down. Daniels inched forward and finished the job. She chose to sit on the sofa beside Tony.

He took his cup and leaned back, his right arm spreading along the back of the sofa. When she leaned back, he closed his arm around her shoulder, bringing her closer to him. There was a prolonged silence before she finally spoke.

"I don't recognize the voice."

"What about the wording?" Tony asked. He felt her shiver and hated the bastard, whoever he was.

"Same as the note with the chocolates," Daniels said.

"It's been weeks. Why now? What's the significance?"

"I don't know. I've been trying to figure it out." Vaughn closed her eyes but didn't move away from his touch.

"I'm going to take the phone and have the message analyzed, see if I can find out anything else. If the voice was computer enhanced. I've got the call being traced, but I wouldn't hold my breath." He fished in his pocket for a second phone and laid it on the table before her. "Use this while I have this one. The number is printed on the back. It should be untraceable." Daniels paused before adding, "Vaughn, I'm going to have them tap this line. It's the only way to try and find this bastard."

"No!" She leaned forward, putting the mug aside. "This was supposed to be over. This is my new home. I don't want him here."

"We don't know for sure it is him, and if it isn't, then we have another problem, a larger one." Daniels waited to get Vaughn's look before continuing. "Are you sure you want him here?" He tilted his head toward Tony.

"Tony has nothing to do with this, so don't make him a personal issue."

Tony was proud of the way she finally asserted herself. He decided to say nothing to interrupt her moment of courage, or to stall it. Several expressions crossed her features before she continued.

"I'm not going back under. I'm not. I flatly refuse. I'd rather let him get me than live that way again." She hesitated and added, "Maybe you'll get him this time and finally finish all this."

"He's not going to get you, Viv." Daniels froze at his slip, and Tony only raised an eyebrow.

Daniels stood and paced before the fire before picking up her cell phone. "I'm going to tap this line, Vaughn. If you want to make calls to lover boy, use the cell I gave you."

"It's already tapped, isn't it?" Tony said. He and Daniels glared at each other.

Vaughn refused to acknowledge the look. "What about my parents?"

"Don't call them unless you do it from the office, as usual. I'll call your dad and tell him to keep alert but not to upset your mother. It shouldn't be a problem. It hasn't in the past."

"What will you tell him?" Tony asked.

"Just that her cell phone was breached. I'll give him my number so we can stay in contact."

"Daniels, what if it's not him? What if it's a crazed radio listener or somebody I've met since I moved here?"

"It's a possibility. We'll check the old sources just to make sure."

"For now if you need her, use the cell you just gave her. I'm taking her out of here for a while." Tony stood and reached for her hand. She slipped her small soft one into his, and Daniels turned away.

"Any chance I could talk you into a short vacation?" Daniels pulled on his jacket and gloves.

Vaughn stood close to Tony and told him no, explaining about her renewed contract. He gave her a halfhearted congratulations they all knew he didn't mean.

"I'm not running anymore. The building is reasonably secure. I can't do it again."

"All right for now, but watch your back. Change whatever kind of routine you've maintained in the last months."

"I know the drill," she told him, the weariness evident in her voice.

Daniels left, and Tony only stopped to grab her new cell phone. He waited while she fumbled with keys and alarmed the door. She didn't ask where he was taking her. He walked her to his door, quickly unlocked it, and pulled her inside. He guided her to the sofa and gently pushed her down by her shoulders.

Chapter Seven

Vaughn closed her eyes in the dark room. Her evening wasn't going to go according to her plan. That was probably the problem—she'd planned so much. Now the reality of her past had come back to haunt her. She could hear Tony moving around in the kitchen but didn't have the energy to find out what he was doing.

He came back with two glasses of wine and thankfully didn't turn on any lights. He handed her one and paused to flip on the fireplace. The warmth of the gas flames made her cozy down into the corner of his sofa. He sat beside her, pulling her against him.

He didn't ask any questions. He waited until she was ready to talk. He left her twice while they sipped the wine. Each time after, she heard a loud beeping in the kitchen. Returning the second time, he asked if she was hungry. She wasn't, and he didn't push. He simply sat beside her, holding her close.

She had known sooner or later she would have to explain all the discrepancies in her past. If she'd fallen for another man, it might not have had to be in such detail. He was a detective, retired or otherwise, and he'd now seen her go to pieces three times. He'd want the truth, and he deserved it.

While she couldn't find the words, she finally pulled the scarf from her neck and opened the top two buttons on her shirt. She moved away and turned on the table lamp beside her. Sitting straight, her legs crossed in front of her, she took a deep breath.

While she gathered her courage to speak, Tony whispered, "You don't have to tell me."

"Yes, I do. I'm falling in love with you, and that puts you in danger. You have a right to know what being involved with me brings. Cop or not, you could get hurt. I don't want that to happen." Admitting her feelings for him hadn't been planned but was honest. If he didn't know all about her, she couldn't expect him to love her.

"I'm not going to let anybody hurt me, or you, Vaughn. I can protect us both if I know what I'm dealing with."

"Start with this." She turned so he could see the red scarring on her neck. The two lines stood out prominently on her pale skin. One was a jagged slash, and the second looked like the result of a tracheotomy. Both were healed over.

He traced the lines with his finger but didn't flinch in horror.

"You should have seen me before the second surgery." She folded back her sleeves and stretched her arms forward. The long slice on each followed just above her wrist line. "No, they weren't self-inflicted." She started to cover the red scars, and he stopped her.

"I'm not horrified, Vaughn. You haven't seen my battle scars yet."

The thought hadn't entered her mind that he'd been wounded too. The idea took her to a different place. "Show me," she whispered.

"Later. You first. You're more important."

"At one time in my life, I thought so too, but then I

realized I'm really insignificant in the grand scheme of things." She handed him her empty glass and waited until he returned with the bottle and refilled both their glasses. In her own time, she spoke. "A long time ago I was just a normal girl, woman. God, it seems like three lifetimes ago." She sipped at the fruity wine to moisten her lips and to buy time to put her thoughts in order. "I grew up in Texas, just outside Austin."

"You don't have any accent."

"I had a long time to perfect overcoming it. Hush and listen because I might not get the courage again to say this." Tony nodded his understanding. "I had a good life. My parents were great. My dad was Austin PD, Mom a PTA mother, the ideal American dream.

"I went to the state university but couldn't decide what I wanted to do. I thought about going on to law school but wasn't sure. So I took some basic courses and got a job with a prestigious law firm. I figured a year working there would help me decide if I wanted to go further.

"I was just a secretary, an assistant pushing deeds and wills through the word processor and beginning to hate it. I was trying to decide what to try next. I know that sounds crazy, but I had the luxury of being young, just twenty-two, and my parents supported my decisions. They just wanted me to find my niche." She drew a deep breath.

"On a regular Friday night, I stayed at work late. I was supposed to meet friends at a club near the office. I'd brought clothes to change into instead of driving home and back. I worked a little later than usual and had just come out of the ladies' room and was ready to leave when I heard an argument." She paused and sipped her wine. "I knew there were still a few people in the office and didn't think much about it. Would you believe I stopped at my desk and fixed my makeup? Sat right there in the hallway outside my bosses' office and fixed my lipstick and blush. The lighting was better." She shook her head at the memory.

"I was so young, so brash. I never believed anything bad could happen to me. The argument got louder." She hesitated, the visual solid before her gaze. "The problem was that to leave I had to pass the office it was coming from. I decided to just hurry past, but something stopped me. To this day I know the timing sucked, and it's what ultimately put me in this position. There have been so many times I've wondered what if. If I'd left earlier? If I hadn't stopped to fix my lipstick? If I hadn't wanted to party on a Friday night? It becomes mind boggling after a while and a huge waste of time. There is no going back to change it."

She picked up the wine, though she didn't want it. The action bought her a few seconds to get her thoughts straight. She put down the glass. "I saw light glinting off something and paused behind the half-closed door to look. It was a gun, and it was pointed at the senior partner, Packard Allen. There were two other men in the room, one holding the gun and one standing beside him. I wasn't sure what the argument was about, but when I went to move on, I heard the second man tell Packard he'd made a mistake, a big mistake. They bantered back and forth a few times, Packard telling him it was all a misunderstanding, that he could explain if Reno just gave him time."

Tony stilled, the name Reno shaking him. She saw the recognition and continued.

"Reno Dawson. You know the name, and now your mind is reeling trying to put it all together." She smiled at him and leaned forward to brush her lips against his. "Reno told him he was right. It was a misunderstanding and all on his part. I'll never forget it. He looked at the other man, a hulk of a body, like a moving, breathing refrigerator. He didn't really have a neck. His head just rested on these huge shoulders. He shot Packard Allen. One shot, directly between the eyes."

She closed her eyes, visualizing the scene again. "I watched him slump back into his chair as if he were in slow motion. Only a single red drip ran down his forehead."

Tony drew her close. "That's enough for tonight, Vaughn."

She pulled away from him and sat straight-backed in her spot in the corner of the couch. "No, let's get it out and over with." She leaned forward and took her glass. Several small sips later, she put down the glass. "To this very day, I don't know how I didn't scream. Reno checked Packard's pulse on his throat to make sure he was dead before they left. I froze, like my feet were embedded in concrete, and that was the thought that made me finally move. That and the sinister laugh Reno let out. I hid under the secretary's desk and waited. They left but never saw me, or I suppose they weren't looking for me. The shot wasn't loud. I waited under the desk until ten o'clock."

She didn't tell him of all the things that went through her mind in the hours she hid. She'd known Packard was dead. Nothing she could have done would change that. What she hadn't realized was that her life had changed the moment the second man pulled the trigger.

"I knew there was a telemarketing firm a few floors below us, and I tried to slip out as if I were one of them, just in case anybody was watching. I didn't go home. I drove three counties over to the police barracks. I went in and told the man at the desk I was having car problems and asked if I could wait there until my father came to get me. He wasn't happy I was there. He told me I should call the auto club, but when I burst into tears, he just pointed to the pay phone and dismissed me. He probably figured I'd had a fight with my boyfriend or something. It didn't matter. I didn't know what else to do." She paused for a deep breath and then a second as the visual memory of the inside of that police station dissolved.

"I knew not to go home, just in case. I called my dad, and he and Mom came to get me. I didn't tell him what was wrong. He knew something bad happened when he heard where I was. An hour later he showed up, flashed his badge, and introduced himself to the desk sergeant. He thanked him for taking care of his daughter and asked if we could leave the car overnight. Again, the sergeant wasn't happy, but at the same time they were changing shifts, so we just slipped out. Dad drove to a little out-of-the-way diner, and we all huddled in a corner booth."

She couldn't turn away from Tony's gaze. The information might kill whatever relationship they were building. If so, better now before they became sexually involved. And she really wanted to become involved in all ways with him. It wasn't the best option, but she had to give him a chance to make his decision with facts, not lust.

"I told them what happened, and we tried to think of a way out of it. There was none. If I didn't tell what I saw and heard, Reno Dawson would get away with ordering my boss's murder. And Mike Elder—the Brick, as they called him—would get away with the actual act. I learned his name later, but the Brick was appropriate."

Tony would understand her dilemma. Having grown up with a father who was a cop, and having been one himself, he knew the position she was in. He also would recognize the position her parents were in. They understood right from the start that evening everything they'd done for their only daughter was gone, washed away in a brief moment she had no control over.

"Jesus, what a hell of a position to be in."

"Tell me about it. I didn't really have a choice. My dad made some calls, and we went directly to the FBI."

"Enough for now. You're shaking, and I'm mad as hell at the injustice of it all." He reached a hand to her and tugged her into the kitchen. "Come on. Let's eat. Too much wine on an empty stomach and all that crap. We can both use a break."

She went willingly, but not for the food, for the diversion.

＊＊＊＊

He placed a steaming bowl of chicken soup in front of her, and she inhaled deeply. After a tentative spoonful, she dug into the thick broth. "Your mother's a great cook," Vaughn told him between bites.

"How do you know I didn't make it?" he teased.

"Woman's intuition." She finished what he served her and refused seconds.

He pushed his empty bowl away, debating what to

do next. He waited for a cue from her and found her smiling. "What?"

"You so want to find out the rest, but you're afraid to traumatize me any further tonight. Thank you for that." She rose and kissed his brow as she gathered up their bowls and took them to the sink. "Thanks, I needed that."

"What would you like to do?" He pulled her down onto his lap. She kissed him long and hard on the lips.

He liked when she took control and would remember to allow her to do it more often.

"Let's go back by the fireplace." She stood and extended her hand.

He followed her lead and sat on the floor beside her in front of the gas flames. He stretched out on his stomach, while she used his ottoman to lean against.

****

"I never saw home again," she said after staring into the flames for a long time. "I never drove my new white Mustang convertible again. I never saw any of my friends again. My parents stayed with me through the first interviews, but the FBI felt it would be better for everyone if they went home and acted as normal as possible." She let out a half laugh, half sigh.

"We made up a story that I eloped over the weekend and my new husband was in the service. I was going to meet him in Japan where he was stationed. They were supposed to make it sound like they were surprised by the whole elopement. It was supposed to be a love-at-first-sight kind of romance, one they didn't even know was happening. My parents were supposed to be happy for me but hesitant about losing their daughter to a virtual stranger who took her halfway across the world for two years. After a few weeks, I handwrote notes to my closest friends, and then the bureau mailed them for me from overseas. It was easy to lose touch after a few letters. Life got busy. The bureau didn't want me to use the internet."

"Did your parents stay in Austin?"

"For a while. My dad took an early retirement, and the program helped them change their last name and relocate. That was my condition. While they didn't go into the program, they helped ease their transition. I go downtown to their offices once a week to call my parents. We all said we were just being careful, that soon I'd be calling them from my cell in the middle of a department store." She stretched and pulled her legs up, hugging her knees. "Now I know that's not a reality." She was thankful he was quiet while she accepted her new reality. Her careful plans for a normal life were dashed with the current reappearance of her stalker. "Anyway, I testified before the grand jury after I calmed down and we got my story straight, and they did the backup legwork to support what I was saying. Reno was so brazen he'd signed in with the security desk because he came in after regular business hours. His own signature basically signed his warrant and that of Mike Elder's."

"How long, Vaughn?"

"Altogether, it's been eight years. Eight long years running and hiding."

"Was that because of the mistrial?"

"Yes. They found out Reno had tampered with the jury, bought off one of them, and the judge had no choice. It took a while to get the second trial together. Motions on both sides, questions about retrying him.

Thank God they had the juror as proof of his involvement, or Reno might still be free today." This time she did sigh. "I'm told that's pretty quick considering we were dealing with several branches of the government and a well-known felon in a highly publicized case. Not to mention Reno's money and friends who 'owed him.' "

"I remember hearing about it, reading about it, but it was so far away."

"And so long ago. I testified during the first trial, and that was enough to keep him looking for me. At first, after the grand jury indictments, we hoped he might cut a deal, but that was wishful thinking. On top of everything, and this was the worst part for me, they let him out on bail between trials." She glanced at Tony and back to the fireplace.

"Of course, it was a lot of money, and they kept his passport so he couldn't leave the country. They used an ankle bracelet to track his movements. Like that would stop a man like Reno Dawson if he really wanted to flee. Somehow, when I'd look at his pictures in the newspaper, he seemed so smug. And there I was, tucked away in little backwater towns, living in places that...that weren't what I was accustomed to. I wanted to work, and they didn't think it was a good idea, too much exposure. There was no justice to it all. My parents settled in Arizona just before I testified." She let out a snort of derision at the memories.

"That was just another injustice, them having to leave the home they'd spent their lives building together, losing their friends and community. Reno partied for years. Between motions and arguments, delays, and everything else that happened, he lived his life to the fullest."

"Where did they hide you?" Tony asked, still stretched out before the flames on his side, his hand holding his head.

"For a while I was in Texas on an abandoned ranch. That was after a year of safe houses all over the general area. They'd get me all settled in some little town with an apartment and sometimes even a part-time job. Then Reno would find me again. It went on like that for six years. Just when I started to feel safe, I'd turn around and a marshal would be at my door. The looks on the marshals' faces said more than their words could. Got any ice cream?"

He laughed at her change of direction. From the kitchen he hollered back he had chocolate or cherry. She opted for the cherry and sat next to him as they ate from the container, sharing the cold cream in front of the fire. When she was sated, she moved back to her spot with her back pressed against the ottoman.

"Where else did you live?" he asked.

"For a while in Georgia, some in Tennessee. The mountain scenery was beautiful. I liked it there. In Arkansas for a while and a few months in New Jersey. I was a waitress, learned to be a reasonable short-order cook, supermarket checker, and a telemarketer. I didn't do well with the marketing."

"What happened next?"

She was getting uncomfortable, and she was thankful he didn't push. He offered her the container again, but she shook her head. How many more times in her life would she have to explain her loneliness and weakness? Today she would have made different choices, but that wouldn't help the past. With Tony, she was taking a chance again. She just hoped her instincts had matured into good sense.

"Just before the second trial was about to start, they brought me back to Texas. I'd met Marcus a few times. He was a city policeman who helped with security occasionally. The marshals knew him, and since they accepted him, I did too." Her voice lagged before she took several breaths. It amazed her that even the memory could still bring her physical pain.

"Unfortunately, I also thought I was in love with him. Most of the men were older, but Marcus was only a few years older than me. He knew who I really was, so I didn't have to pretend with him. The marshals figured I was safe with him. I wasn't naïve, just lonely. He made me feel alive again, made me feel like I still had the chance to have a normal life. Anyway, when it became apparent the second trial was going to continue no matter what attempts Reno and his lawyers tried…"

This was one of the few times since she'd known him that she turned away from him. She stood and moved to his bathroom without comment. She used one of his hand towels to wipe her face and wrists with cold water, hoping it would give her the courage to continue.

When she returned, Tony hadn't moved. She settled beside him, intent on finishing the story. "I had wonderful men who stayed with me. Jacob, the other message on the phone, became a surrogate father to me. The rest of the team had gone into town to get supplies one afternoon and figured it wasn't a problem because Jacob was with me as well as Marcus. The second guard, Williams, had been called away on family business. I never questioned any of it. We needed groceries, and I wasn't going to be alone, no problem.

Only there was a big problem." Vaughn wanted to sigh but held it back.

"God, I was so stupid, so trusting. All Marcus had to do was look at me with those dreamy blue eyes, and I'd melt. It was a Friday evening. There was a baseball game on television. Jacob decided to watch it for a while to give Marcus and me some privacy. He wasn't blind, and he knew—he just knew—we were young and I was falling in love. What he didn't know was who Marcus was really working for."

She stood and started pacing around his apartment. She was thankful Tony let her go, not invading her space. "I was making fudge. Can you believe it—fudge? Marcus went to check the score. I heard a strange noise, but he was right back. I asked if everything was all right, and he said he walked into the coffee table. I turned my back on him. There was a window over the kitchen sink, and I saw his reflection in it, coming toward me. He had a scalpel in his hand, like they'd use to operate on you. Light reflecting off the blade caught my attention." She paused and all but gulped for air. One part of her wanted to stop, but the other side of her knew if she wanted something special with Tony, she would have to trust him. But before that happened, he deserved to know the truth, to know what he was attaching himself to.

"I was stunned. Can you understand that? Downright stunned and outraged at the idea that Marcus would hurt me. I screamed for Jacob, but he didn't answer. Then I knew what the noise was. Marcus had knocked him out. He came at me, apologizing for what he was about to do."

Tony took shallow breaths, forcing back the anger

she read on his expression and in his tight body language.

"I realized he hadn't shot him, or I'd have heard the noise. I figured he'd go back and finish Jacob later, after he'd taken care of me. Somehow, I truly believed he was sorry but not enough not to kill me. I threw the hot pot of chocolate at him, which was a bad idea on many fronts. While it burned him only slightly, it made the floor slippery. We both went down when he lunged for me." She didn't try to hold back the shiver of revulsion that came with the memory.

"He managed to grab my wrists, and then he slit them. I remember feeling my warm blood running down into my hands and dripping off my fingers. I watched as it mixed with the chocolate on the floor. I heard a noise from behind me, and the next thing I knew Marcus shot Jacob. His body hit the floor with a thud." Her body flinched at the memory. "I remember he pulled my mouth to his, and he kissed me goodbye. He actually said 'Goodbye, Vivian' before he ran the blade across my throat. I woke up in the hospital two days later."

"Jesus." Tony stayed where he was, staring at her. "He survived?" he managed to ask, though his voice held an angry edge.

"Jacob survived, but he lost his left eye because of me."

"No, he lost his eye in the line of duty, and it was because of Marcus."

"Semantics, Tony."

"Tell me the rest. Then we'll let it go for a while, all right?"

She understood his need to know the rest. "I spent

two weeks in the hospital and a few more months in a private hospital. After the attack, I pretty much lost it. It was Jacob who made me realize if I didn't get my act together, Reno would win again." She went around the room, straightening stacks of books and paper.

"By then, Marcus had been found on a lonely stretch of back road, in his car, with a single gunshot to the head. His gun was never recovered, and there was no other gun in the car. Later they found out he liked to gamble, and Reno had struck a deal with him. Williams, the other marshal, was new to the team. He disappeared after the incident. In the confusion of getting me and Jacob to the hospital, they realized he'd slipped away, never to be heard from again. Supposedly, he'd been reassigned." She turned to Tony and gave him a small smile.

"They were able to stall the trial until I was competent to testify, and I did, scars and all. It was the last time I went out in public with my scars showing. I walked into the courtroom in a plain white T-shirt. The scars were much more prominent then, still blood red and gruesome. I wanted the jury to see what he'd ordered done to me. It worked. They found Reno guilty of ordering Packard Allen's murder and eventually Mike Elder guilty of the actual shooting. There was another trial about Reno's tampering with the jury and another for Marcus's murder and the attempts on my and Jacob's lives."

"And all the time you had to stay underground." Tony shook his head in disbelief.

"Yes, it was the only way to see it come to fruition."

"Reno is away for life, I presume?"

"Supposedly. Elder got life plus twenty for the two murders, and Reno got a total of one hundred and twenty years to run consecutively. The worst part was he was still allowed out on bail after he was convicted of Packard's murder until the sentencing, and then there were appeals. Again, he was out living his life, and I was hiding away. There never seemed to be much justice in that to me. Obviously, I didn't go on to law school or any other."

"How did you wind up on the radio?" he asked.

"Jacob retired and moved to Seattle. When everything was as settled as it could get, I moved up there for a while. He suggested I try voice-over work. Nobody would see me to recognize me, and after everything Marcus had done, well, it left me with this smoky dark voice, as he calls it."

"What made you come to New York?"

"I knew if I stayed in Seattle, I'd never find a life for myself. It was too easy to lean on Jacob, and that wasn't fair. Two years was as long a safety line as I could give myself. I need to find out who I'd turned into. Vivian Montgomery was long dead in all ways. Vaughn Matthews had to find a way to survive and be responsible for herself again or really for the first time in her life."

Chapter Eight

Tony fisted his hands at his sides. What he'd heard infuriated him. He didn't want to overwhelm her with questions, and he wanted to get his emotions in check. In his twenty years on the force, he'd dealt with the marshals. Clients usually had one main marshal who was responsible for them once they were relocated and settled. With Vaughn, he understood the need to change tactics. He also understood why Jacob felt responsible and had tried to bring her back to as normal a life as she could have.

She stood in the darkened archway, halfway to the door. He stretched leisurely before he rose. Her eyes shimmered with tears, but she didn't let them escape and fall onto her cheeks. His movement had brought her back from the memories.

"Come with me." He reached a hand to her, and she took it, following his lead into his bedroom. She hesitated at the door, and he pulled her in. She stood still for a second, getting acquainted with the space. The room was similar to hers but painted beige with a dark brown paisley spread pulled up over the king-size bed. His bath and closet were on the opposite side from hers. He dragged the heavy spread to the foot of the bed to reveal crisp-looking light blue sheets and pillowcases. He sat on the side of the bed and pulled off his boots.

He took a small revolver from an ankle holster and put it in the nightstand drawer. She watched him, seemingly surprised when he stopped there.

"Vaughn, come lie down for a while. You need to rest."

"But I thought…" She looked defeated.

"Not tonight. I want us to be alone together. No memories, all right? I just want you to stay close to me tonight. I promise you'll be safe." He watched her for a long time as she made up her mind.

She nodded to the bathroom and closed the door behind her. When she came out, she sat beside him on the bed and kicked off her shoes. She stood and tugged off her jeans, slipping down onto the closest pillow still half-dressed.

Tony let out a sigh as he dropped his jeans and stripped off his T-shirt. He moved behind her, pulling her to spoon against the length of his body, leaving his arm draped over her waist. "Comfortable?"

"Yes."

"Why does Jacob call you Blondie?"

She let out a little laugh, and he knew she was back in the room with him. "When this first happened, I was young, lots of makeup and blonde hair."

"You, a blonde? I don't see it," he teased, his breath against her ear. The movement caused the hairs around her ear to move, and her hand brushed them away. It lingered a bit to trace his jawline.

"I was a blonde when Reno and the Brick killed Packard. For a while I was a redhead, mostly while living in Tennessee. I went from white blonde to jet black. But I never revealed my natural brown hair back then. I suppose even then I knew I'd want to keep some parts of Vivian."

"I'd like to meet Jacob someday, thank him for taking care of you and for helping you."

"I'd like you to meet him too. In some ways, even though it's awful to admit, we're closer than I am with my own father."

"A matter of circumstance, not choice, Vaughn. Do you hate being called by your new name?" He felt her relax against him, her breathing patterned.

"Not really. It was better than Virginia or Veta. And I didn't feel like a Valerie. I knew a Valerie once. She was very peppy and happy all the time. I wasn't. I didn't feel like a Violet or Veronica. I never knew anyone named Vaughn. I could create her."

"I like what you've done so far," he whispered as she fell asleep.

****

"I like what you've done so far," Tony had whispered as she fell asleep.

It was the first thing she remembered when she woke in the early hours of the morning, the light just starting to stream through the blinds Tony hadn't closed last night. She snuggled against his back, her arm wrapped around his waist. Carefully untangling herself from him, she pushed the hair from her face and took a look around. The masculine room fit him. She was torn between slipping out of bed and going home or staying beside him. His warmth won out. That was when she realized she'd never spent the night with a man. She'd dated but never spent the night. Of course, in those days she still lived at home.

The few stolen moments with Marcus were always just that, small patches of time she could be unaccounted for.

She was surprised she wasn't nervous with Tony. She rolled onto her other side, and he rolled closer, pulling her to him.

"Don't go," he whispered dreamily.

No verbal answer was needed as she tucked herself against him. A short time later she let her imagination run wild. With him behind her, she couldn't go back to sleep, not with the ideas of how to love him swirling inside her. Her hand slipped back between them, exploring. He'd kept his boxers on, and she slipped her hand down his thigh, feeling the texture of his muscles.

"If you keep doing that, I'm not going to be responsible for what happens next. Go back to sleep, Vaughn."

"I don't think so, Anthony Lombardo the Fifth." She'd woken up with Vaughn Matthews's attitude toward life. She was bold and brash and went for what she wanted. Vaughn turned in his arms and let her hands wander along his naked chest. He was pretending to be asleep, the corners of his lips giving him away while her fingers teased his bare skin. His cock grew against her, his control all but lost.

"We are quickly approaching a point of no return," he said through gritted teeth.

The palm of her hand found him warm and hard through the opening in the front of his boxers. "I know." She eased down to explore him. With a light push, she rolled him onto his back, his morning erection presenting itself. "Oh, Tony, you're beautiful," she told him just before she slipped down and became intimately acquainted with him. She instinctively backed off, prolonging his release. She teased him several times before moving up his body, her hair running across his bare chest.

"Where's the protection?" she asked, her voice low and still sleepy. She teased his ear with her tongue and felt the shiver work through him. He pointed to the nightstand, and she straddled his chest, reaching over. His hands came up to support her and slipped under her shirt.

His large fingers weren't meant to undo a lady's shirt. He made several attempts at the bottom button, gave up, and grabbed the hem. He pulled it up and off her in one long tug.

She laughed as she brushed the hair from her face while she leaned down to kiss him. Morning breath didn't deter her. He ran his hands along her torso, only stopping when he came in contact with the lace bra.

His hands ran along the back, and she pulled his fingers to cup her breasts. She snapped open the small plastic front clasp, freeing herself from the underwire torture device. Tony's hands slipped onto her naked skin and took her weight into his palms, gently rubbing her where wire had chafed her delicate skin. She reveled in the way he brought her nipples to attention.

Tony let out a groan and pulled himself up against the headboard, taking her with him. His mouth engulfed first one hard peak and then the other, a delicious torture she was enjoying. Grinding against him, she knew she was ready.

"Tony, please?"

"Please what?"

Vaughn squirmed back, trying to get closer to his erection. Frustrated that he knew what she wanted and wasn't letting her have him, she tore open the foil package and twisted out of his grasp. Her lips found him again before she finally encased him. She slipped off her panties and dropped her weight onto him, relishing in the stretch her body made to accommodate him.

At first, she thought to tease them both, lowering in increments onto him, but when the moment came, she wanted to be filled. When he was deeply embedded inside her, she stopped to catch her breath. His dark eyelashes shadowed against his cheeks. She brought her lips to his and sucked his tongue into her mouth as she started the slow ritual movements that drove him to a crazed pitch.

She sensed Tony was on a short leash and was going to lose control any second. His hands left her breasts and found her face, pulling her momentarily away from him.

"God, Vaughn." He thrust up inside her as he kissed her deeply. His hands dropped to her hips and held her against his upward movement. Her muscles clamped around him, tighter if it was possible, and he lost all control.

She had been alone a long time, and she wanted her release, but the place Tony took her was new. She'd never reached this level, and she liked it. She wanted more, now. Her arms were wrapped around his head, her head lying on top of his. Small, quick movements of her hips had her teasing him back to life. He allowed her to control him a while longer before he grasped her waist and rolled her under him.

Looking up into his dark eyes, she smiled. Being with Tony felt right, as if she'd finally found home. He studied her face with each thrust and retreat, learning what she liked and where. Simple sighs, laughs, and roaming hands became their conversation. Letting her eyes slip closed, she felt safe and loved for the first time in her adult life.

Chapter Nine

Tony would lose control if he kept this up, and he didn't want to lose her just yet. He pulled from inside her and slid back until he was nestled between her thighs, to sate her temporarily. The heat they created made him harder. Slipping his index finger inside her, he felt her pulse around it, and he sucked harder, feeling her spasm.

Instinct had him reaching for fresh protection before he lost his edge, lost the idea of bringing her more pleasure, and he mounted her quickly. In one long push he was back inside her, and her eyes opened wide to watch him, to connect with him.

She urged him on. "Hurry, Tony, faster." Her fingers bit into his waist, holding him tight to her. "Go deeper…"

He lost his ability to control himself any longer and shifted her against him. She tightened in response, as if her insides were made of pulsing velvet, and he stopped resisting. When he finally lowered her hips to the bed, it took all his strength not to drop on top of her.

"Jesus, Vaughn, are you trying to kill me before I marry you?" he teased. They both froze at his words.

She started to snicker. Finally, she let out a full laugh. "God, you should have seen the look on your face. All this dark olive skin went pale white."

He let himself down beside her, begrudgingly

pulling from inside her. He rolled away momentarily to toss the used protection and came back, his fingers running along her flat belly.

"I'm so glad I could brighten your morning," he told her before diving toward her breast, his lips sucking her deep into his mouth. His finger dipped easily inside her and mimicked the motions his mouth made.

She groaned, tightened, and exploded once again, seemingly without shame or embarrassment. He worked her through the peak and long into the valley before taking his hand and lips from her body. When he did, he brushed the hair from her forehead and dropped a light kiss on her temple.

"I need coffee." It was a blatant statement of fact.

"Yes, ma'am. Any other wants I can satisfy at the moment?" He grinned at her.

She gave him a sly smile. "Actually, several, but I'll give you some time to recoup your energy."

He tossed a pillow in her direction as he slowly crawled over her. He paused to enjoy a few moments of body contact before leaving the bed.

"Tony?"

He stopped several feet from her, not embarrassed by his nakedness. "What?"

"Come back for a second," she whispered. She extended her hand to him.

He paused a few inches before she could reach him, and he leaned over. "What?" He knew what she wanted, or at least he thought he did. She asked him to turn around, and he knew for sure. He slowly turned and lowered himself onto the side of the bed. He knew she was looking at his battle scar. Her finger traced the path of the uneven line that ran from his shoulder blade diagonally to the corner of his back.

"Tonight, we can discuss your war stories." She placed a line of small kisses along the raised skin. It was a strangely intense moment, almost more intimate than their lovemaking had been, on a different level. "But one thing…"

"What?" His hand reached to take hers, clasped on his shoulder.

"What does a girl have to do to get a cup of coffee around here?"

He shook his head, laughing as he pulled away. "She merely has to ask," he told her as he finally padded away from the bed.

In the kitchen, Tony turned on his ever-ready coffee pot and let the counter support his weight. He was in deep, and he knew it. There was no turning back. When he slipped earlier, he'd meant it. He was going to marry Vaughn Matthews. It was a given in his mind. Making her want the same thing might take some convincing.

He walked slowly back to the bedroom, a mug of hot coffee in each hand. She stood by the windows, her naked back to him. She was beautiful in all ways, inside and out. She gave herself freely and was woman enough to accept what he offered her. He became semierect at the sight of her.

"Your coffee as requested," he said with a smile, not wanting to scare her from her thoughts.

She turned, smiling, and met him halfway across the room. She sat on the edge of the bed, both her hands wrapped around the mug as if to warm them.

He sat beside her, pulling the blanket up around her

shoulders. "Cold?"

"Hopefully not for long," she answered with a glint in her eye. After taking a tentative sip of the coffee, she let out a sigh similar to one he'd heard earlier this morning. "I admit it—you make wonderful coffee."

"Thank you." They were both quiet, sipping from their mugs. His arm was still around her shoulders, holding the blanket in place. He wasn't sure where to go from here. Every woman was different, and it had been a long time since he had a woman stay overnight. He was out of practice with what the morning-after protocol was these days.

Vaughn broke the silence. "Can I ask you something, Tony?"

"Anything." He pressed his lips to the soft spot behind her ear.

"What happens now? I mean…oh hell, I've never woken up in a man's apartment before."

His outright laughter wasn't confidence inspiring, and he saw the look on her face. "Oh, angel, I'm so glad to hear that. I know it's not politically correct to think it—let alone say it aloud—but I'm glad. I figure we should just make it up as we go along. As long as we're both comfortable, we'll find our way together."

"Does together include a hot shower, or am I supposed to go home now?" Turning to face him, she handed him her empty mug; her arms slid around his neck, her lips to his collar bone.

"It definitely includes a hot shower, but if you keep that up, we're not going to make it to one for a while." He pulled out of her embrace and moved to the bureau. He put the two mugs down and reached for her hand. She went willingly with him. He was intrigued by all the new adventures that lay ahead.

****

He'd gone home with her later that afternoon. He couldn't force her to stay with him. Their morning together had turned into a sensory experience he'd never forget. He'd never look at his shower again without remembering how she'd touched him, physically and emotionally.

They'd made breakfast together and made love afterward. They'd made lunch together and made love afterward. Each time the depth and intensity of their acts surprised him. She'd begrudgingly told him it was time to head home. She'd nap for a while and get ready for work.

Tony remembered the look on her face when he told her he'd take her to the station. Surprise had turned to confusion and then anger. "I'll see you to the radio station when you're ready." Wasn't that what boyfriends were supposed to do?

"No, you won't."

"Yes, I will." He tried to persuade her with a kiss.

She pulled from his embrace. "No, you won't. Just because we had sex doesn't make you my new keeper." Her tone made him believe she was beyond pissed off.

"We didn't have sex. We made love numerous times, and I'm not your keeper, just…"

"Just what, Tony?"

She stared at him, and he knew he'd lost the argument when he blinked first.

"*Men.*" She threw her arms up. "A little sex and they think they own you. I'm in charge of me, Mr. Lombardo, and it will stay that way. I don't need an egotistical male with raging hormones any more than I need to be coddled."

"But, Vaughn, under the circumstances..." He hesitated to reach for her, knowing he walked a very fine line between his temper and hers.

"No, Tony. You can keep your antiquated theories of gallantry and shove them up your ass. As a matter of fact, you can fuck yourself with them too!"

He only managed to stop the tirade of four-letter words by kissing her hard on the mouth.

"I get you're capable of getting to and from work on your own. And I admit it bothers me just a little that you are so self-sufficient."

She pressed her hips hard against his for just a second. "It bothers you just a little," she had teased, edging them from what might have become an argument.

Only now, hours later and waiting for her to sign on the air, did he realize how much she needed to do the small everyday things most people took for granted.

He'd been genuinely surprised when his phone rang an hour later. She'd thanked him for an emotional evening and a wonderful morning and hedged around the cold weather before admitting the call was to let him know she had arrived safely. Making the call had taken courage on many levels, and he was secretly pleased she'd thought of him. After all they'd joked, he'd know in a little while when she signed on the air.

Now the problem was how to sleep without her beside him. He'd been an insomniac for years, naps getting him by. But in the months since he'd been listening to her nightly show, he'd found consecutive hours of sleep. They'd showered twice together, and he still carried her scent on his skin. It was embedded in his brain forever.

Lying there, he knew he wouldn't sleep. He got up and moved to the desk, where he switched on the lights and gathered the files. He glanced up at the photos he'd hung and remembered his earlier conversation with Vaughn.

After breakfast, she'd asked him about the case. He'd told her it was still cold and would probably stay that way. Though he'd spent weeks retracing each statement and fact, nothing changed. Vaughn studied the photos and spoke her thoughts without censoring them, something he liked and abhorred about her. But he wouldn't change her bluntness for anything. She earned that right one hundred times over to be...herself. Now was especially important because she was finding her true self.

"Danielle was a handsome woman, wasn't she? I mean, beautiful but not in a fluffy sort of way. Her eyes have a sadness about them I can't explain. Look. Even in the wedding photo, she's smiling, but there's sadness behind her smile."

He joined her at the desk and tried to see what she saw. They agreed that Danielle was handsome, not beautiful in standard advertising terms. He pulled the age-enhanced photo from the folder. The Rimons had the composite done two years before he got the file. He showed it to Vaughn, and she laughed aloud.

"If the woman in these photos looks anything like that, I'd be completely surprised. This is too prissy, too feminine."

He understood what she meant but still couldn't visualize what she was seeing. She pulled the wedding photo forward and leaned it against the lamp, taking a step back to look at it again.

"She just looks so...frozen in place. That's not correct, though." She spread them all in chronological order. "See what I mean? Every formal portrait is forced. Only the candids are relaxed."

"Most people don't take great pictures."

"I know, but it's like she's trying to be what she's supposed to be, not who she really is. Trust me, Tony. I'm the perfect one to see that. I spent too many years of my life being what other people wanted me to be."

She sorted the pictures into two separate piles. She spread the formal shots on the desk and took the candids to the coffee table, where she laid them in chronological order. Then she took a step back and went from the desk to the table several times.

"It's like looking at two separate women. Here, these on the table, she's happy in her jeans and sweats. But here, in dresses and formal wear, she's uncomfortable. That's what I see, Tony. She's uncomfortable in the skin she wears for her family and outsiders. She's mixed when with her husband. Only in the candids does she seem relaxed and at peace."

He began to see what she meant. Separating the photos had been an act of genius. "If I ever figure out what happened, I'm going to have to give you half my fee." His arms went around her waist, pulling her back against him.

"Maybe you should make me your partner. We can at least write off the overhead."

She laughed, but he knew truer words had never been spoken. In time, he hoped she'd see his side and let herself love him unconditionally. Neither of them had mentioned the marriage comment the rest of the day, but for him it was a new reality to work toward.

****

Tonight when Tony heard her voice telling him he wasn't alone in the night, he thought back to Danielle and wondered if she was alive, if she was alone. It brought back an earlier observation Vaughn had made. She asked if any female friends had moved or gone missing around the same time.

He took the file to his chair and reached for his glasses. With them firmly in place on his nose, he started on the first report and went through the folder again. This time, he was two-thirds of the way through when he found a notation about a woman, Helen Martin, from the same accounting firm, moving four weeks earlier. He moved to his computer and started pulling up sites. A short time later, he found what he was looking for.

Helen Martin was listed under CPAs. She lived and worked in a small town near Hunter Mountain, New York. He was familiar with the ski area, even though he wasn't a skier. He had no photograph of her and figured it might be worth it to take a ride up there and see if Ms. Martin knew anything about Danielle. He used an old backdoor password from his days on the force to access the DMV and printed a copy of her driver's license for reference. He was surprised the password still worked. Vaughn should go with him. He was following her lead, and it would be a nice day's drive for them.

Vaughn surprised him early the next morning. Just before seven, she knocked on his door, a bag of hot bagels in her hand. He brushed the sleep from his eyes as he opened the door. He automatically pulled her to him. The cold coming from her coat gave him a chill, and she teased she could warm him up.

She stripped while walking through his apartment, draping her coat and scarf over the sofa. She paused to toe off her boots and dropped them by the desk. Her pants and sweater missed the bed as she pulled them off and bypassed him to turn on the shower. Running the water and waiting for it to get hot, she moved back, tugging at the waist of his sweatpants until they were down his hips. His cock embarrassingly bobbed to life before her.

He managed to kick the pants off as he unhooked her bra and filled his hands with her naked breasts. She turned in the bathroom doorway to kiss him, the kiss he'd thought about all night. Directing him to the shower, she followed him under the hot spray of water.

Her early morning visit surprised him, but his body was ready. The ache he'd felt all night and couldn't place was because she wasn't with him. He'd have to be careful with his wants until she was more comfortable around him. He turned his thoughts to the present, pulling her against him.

Her kiss inspired him, and he took her arms and held them over her head, controlling her movements, cautiously at first until she relaxed into the act. He sucked one nipple into his mouth and then the other and felt her struggle to free her hands. He pulled away from her breast and dragged her arm to his mouth, his tongue running along the scar on each wrist. She shook under his touch, and he did it again, dropping her arms on his shoulders and lifting her onto his waiting length. She wrapped her legs tightly around his hips.

Her arms held him tight. With her back pressed

against the tiled wall, she took every stroke he gave her and wanted more. When he pushed her over the edge into the abyss, he followed along with her, quickly pulling his cock from her body since he wasn't wearing a condom. His muscles quaked to hold both their weights. Slowly, he lowered her to the floor and back under the warm spray. "We're going to have to keep a stash of condoms in here."

"Good morning to you too," she whispered before taking the soap from the ledge and lathering his body. Her soapy hands slid across him, and his eyes slipped closed.

Chapter Ten

Vaughn slept away most of the short drive. Tony had picked her up at the station, with two hot cups of coffee waiting in the console for them. She'd dozed, obviously confident with him behind the wheel. When he reached the outskirts of town, she came awake, as if some sixth sense were letting her know they were near.

"Morning. We're here already. I'm sorry I fell asleep."

"No problem. We're just coming into town. How about we stop for breakfast? My appointment with Ms. Martin isn't until ten thirty."

"Sounds good to me, and you can run over our cover story again while we eat."

He smiled. When he'd told her of his find, he'd credited her for it. After all, he told her, her thoughts made him look differently at the evidence again. He found a small café, and while they devoured huge plates of pancakes and sausage, he reinforced his plan. They found the offices with ease and were fifteen minutes early.

Helen Martin walked from the rear office, her tweed slacks and bulky knit sweater making her look heavier than she probably was. She introduced herself to them and shook both his and Vaughn's hands with two hearty pumps. They followed her to her private office and settled across the desk from her.

"Thank you for agreeing to meet with us, Ms. Martin," Tony started.

"Please call me Helen. Everyone does. Now when you phoned, you mentioned you were thinking about relocating here, but you didn't mention what sort of business you'd be starting."

Tony and Vaughn listened to her talk about incentives for certain types of businesses and answered her questions as if they wanted to start a restaurant. He listened for several minutes, but Vaughn interrupted the meeting. She'd stood and stretched a few moments earlier and walked to the window behind Helen. From there, she could see the photos on Helen's desk.

The look on her face was all he needed to see. They both knew instantly, and so did Helen. She stopped talking midsentence and stared at him.

"You're not interested in opening a restaurant, are you, Mr. Lombardo?"

He leaned forward, his hand reaching to his computer case beside his seat. He pulled out a photo of Danielle and handed it across the desk. "I'm a private investigator. Do you know the woman in the photo? Her name is Danielle Rimon-Aubin. She's been missing for years. You both worked at the same accounting firm for two years prior to her disappearance. You relocated one month before her disappearance."

Helen pushed a strand of brown hair behind her ear and leaned back in her seat.

"May I?" Vaughn asked, now back across the desk in her seat. She nodded to the photograph she'd spotted and handed the frame to Tony.

He tried to hold back the astonished look that crossed his face, knowing he wasn't doing a good job of it.

The woman in the photo was Danielle. Her hair was cropped shorter, and she'd gained some weight. The smile on her face surprised him. In all the photographs he'd seen of Danielle, there was an inherent sadness. Vaughn had been right. This one, however, was different. She smiled brightly, her eyes twinkling for the camera. The word that came to his mind was *content*.

"I've been telling her for years she should have told them."

All at once, Helen lost control. Tears trickled down her cheeks, and a sob escaped from her throat. Vaughn went to her, hugging her until she was able to control herself.

"What are you going to do?" Helen reached for a tissue to blow her nose.

It was a hearty blow, not a feminine wipe, and Tony decided he liked her. She was what she was, and because of him, now she was afraid. Her future was about to come crashing down on her.

"I'd like to talk to Danielle. I was hired by her parents to find her. All this time they've held out hope she was alive, and if she wasn't, they've blamed George Aubin."

"I'll take you to her," she told them with a sigh.

They bundled up in their winter coats and gloves. Tony couldn't believe how smoothly this was going. In his experience, most people tended to run for cover or at least run away when confronted. Helen hadn't. She seemed to accept the inevitable.

Outside, the sun warmed the late-winter morning, but the snow piled on the sides of the road gave off cold air around them. He motioned Helen toward his SUV parked a few doors away, and she only shook her head. After they crossed the street, they headed down the block until they came to a small art gallery.

Its windows held both paintings and photographs. There were several small metal sculptures on black-velvet-covered pedestals interspersed with photos and watercolors on easels of varying heights. A sign in the lower corner told anyone passing by that custom framing was their specialty.

As Helen pushed open the door, a string of reindeer bells notified anyone in the shop they had company. From a back room a short, stocky woman dressed in worn overalls and a thick, quilted flannel shirt greeted them, drying her hands on a paper towel.

"How can I help you folks today?" she asked brightly until she saw Helen standing with them. Her face went blank, and she froze in place.

He knew they were standing in front of Danielle. Vaughn's squeezing his hand suggested she knew too. Yes, Danielle had aged and gained some weight, but it was definitely her. Helen went to her, and she slumped against her body. He glanced at Vaughn. He hated that he had ruined their perfect life. Whatever halcyon years they shared, their lives would never be the same. He was sorry he'd completed his task.

"We knew it might happen one day," Helen told her.

"I know. I suppose it's best to get it over with. But..." Danielle hugged her life partner closer to her body before she pulled back and rested her forehead against Helen's. "The other shoe dropped," she said, and they laughed together through tears. She sobered and stared at Helen. "I'm glad. I can divorce George, and we can finally get married." She smiled and laughed, and after several seconds of realization, Helen joined her.

Like a voyeur, Tony watched the moment. His years of police training deserted him. He cleared his throat to gain their attention.

"Dani, this is Tony and Vaughn Lombardo," Helen said. "He's a private investigator your parents hired."

He watched both women get themselves together before Dani moved forward to him, her hand extended. He didn't correct her about their names or marital status, and neither did Vaughn.

"Dani Martin," she started, then paused. "All our careful planning and hiding in plain sight is over."

"I'm sorry, but your parents are—"

"Going to be furious, I know." She moved away and walked behind one of the counters. She pulled a wooden stool closer and sat heavily. With her elbows on the glass counter, she used the balls of her hands to relieve the pressure mounting in her temples. He used the same motion when his head ached.

Helen disappeared only to return shortly with a can of soda and a bottle of generic aspirin.

"I know this is going to sound crazy, but I've been checking on them. I get the local paper delivered and…" Dani burst into tears again.

Tony looked to Vaughn, who just shook her head. She moved forward and reached a hand across to the woman who was obviously torn between her old life and her new.

"Dani, I won't presume to know what your life was like in Philadelphia, but your parents have blamed

George all these years. Two years ago he gave up on finding you and started living his life then. Can you understand that? When he petitioned the court to declare you dead, he'd spent years of his life looking for you, waiting for you, wondering what happened to you. You owe it to him and your parents to let them know, even if it's just that you're alive. We're not asking you to go back."

Vaughn turned to Tony, questioning him with her eyes. "Do you have to tell her parents where she is? Could she just call and talk to them?"

For the first time, he saw hope in Dani's and Helen's faces. Did Vaughn realize the position she'd put him in?

She moved closer and took his hand, drawing him toward the front of the shop. "I'm sorry. I didn't mean to... It's just if she was so unhappy to go to these lengths... Do you have to tell her parents where she is? Technically, if she called them..."

He ran his hand through his hair, and she smiled coyly.

"I apologize. I was supposed to come along for the ride, not make your job harder."

He shook his head, understanding what she wanted to hear him say. But his job was to find out what happened to Danielle, and now he had. In the other two cold cases he'd worked, both persons were known dead. Their killers were the people he found. It was clear-cut, with no question as to what had to be done. Evidence was gathered, handed over to the right persons, and the arrest was made. This situation treaded on some mighty murky waters.

"Let's all go someplace and have a cup of coffee,"

he said, "and see what we can figure out." He interpreted the looks on all three women's faces as relief.

Dani locked the shop door and flipped the Closed sign. Then they all went into the back work area, where Helen pulled four sodas from the small refrigerator under a worktable.

****

Their story wasn't anything new. He'd heard it before in a hundred different versions, each with its own personal twist. For Danielle Rimon-Aubin, the pressure to always be the perfect little girl with hair ribbons and lacy dresses weighed heavily upon her when she really wanted to climb trees and play in the mud. Her parents doted on their only daughter, wanting everything feminine. Sports were supposed to be tennis and swimming, not basketball and soccer.

"I was never really comfortable with men. George was different. He was a gym teacher and coach. When I was around him, I didn't have to be prissy, because he accepted me as I was." She sighed loudly and wiped her eyes with a tissue. "I married George as a last resort. My parents were parading suitable men in and out of the house all the time." Her exasperated voice continued. "There was never an option of leaving home before marriage. They never allowed me to think about having an apartment of my own, even after I finished college. I only went to State because I could commute. They refused to let me board, even though I had full scholarships." She glanced at Helen and gave her a special smile, one Tony accepted as private between them.

"They thought George was beneath us, but at least

129

he had a reputable job with the high school, and *at least* I would be married. That's what they wanted. I was supposed to marry and live according to their perception of a perfect home, family, and marriage. Even though the rest of the world was adapting, my parents' attitude would never change. They often made rude comments on the topic. Their beliefs were set in stone.

"We became good friends, but physically, his equipment didn't excite me. I'd known for years my preference was women, but I couldn't tell them since I'd disappointed them so many times already. I had been thinking about a divorce, but my parents would never allow it. Not unless I could say George had done something wrong, and I couldn't do that to him either. He married me with good intentions." Danielle blushed. "Then Helen came to work at the firm, and we forged a fast friendship that led to an intimate relationship."

They clasped their fingers tighter. He remembered the photo from the softball team and knew where he'd seen Helen before.

Danielle steadied herself and continued. "Once I understood there was nothing really wrong with me, I knew I couldn't stay. I was the one who broke my marriage vows."

"We made our plans carefully," Helen added.

Tony glanced at Vaughn, who was intent on hearing their story.

"We made sure it was a day when George would be accounted for so there wouldn't be any speculation about him." Her voice dropped to almost a whisper. "As to my parents, I just couldn't find the courage to tell them the truth. They were so disappointed over the years, and I couldn't bear to tell them the truth." She straightened and pulled herself together. "I walked away from my old life and started fresh with Helen."

"You have to remember back then being gay or lesbian wasn't as accepted as it is now. We never dreamed one day we'd have the same right to marriage. Never." Helen sniffed back her threatening tears and rising voice. "We've built a good life together, except for the guilt we share only with each other. Holidays are the hardest on Dani."

Tony listened and garnered the small details from their conversation. He pushed back in his seat, his hand now rubbing his temples.

"Mr. Lombardo, technically, I haven't broken any laws, right? I was over twenty-one, and I wanted to get away from their preconceived notions. I know I hurt them and George too, but if I go back, will I face charges of any kind?"

"Since she walked away, she's never even opened a bank account," Helen added. "She didn't falsify any records or borrow a social security number. Technically, she's been in limbo for the missing time."

"Helen owns the shop and everything else we've built together," Dani said.

He realized the amount of courage it took to be herself. He remembered meeting her parents. While they were very proper, he'd attributed their anxiety to the situation. Now he was beginning to see it from Dani's side. He wouldn't have wanted to go up against them under most circumstances, and he'd only met them twice. How had Dani managed all those years, living a life they expected from her when she was somebody else inside, fighting to hide from the pressure?

"Before we debate this any further, I think it would be best to contact a lawyer, see where you stand legally." It was the best he could do for them under the circumstances.

****

Tony took Vaughn for a tour of the area, openly wondering if Dani and Helen would be at the office when they went back at the agreed-upon three o'clock. He was relieved when Helen unlocked the door.

"We spoke briefly with an associate, and he feels there could be some repercussions," she said immediately.

"Technically, I was an adult who chose not to have any contact with my parents or husband. I had that right. Although now all these years later, I do wish I'd had the courage to be honest. It hasn't been fair to Helen, watching over her shoulder to watch my back.

"The lawyer told us my choices going about it were not in anyone's best interest but my own. By not defrauding anyone all these years, I've simply moved away and failed to give them a forwarding address." Dani almost smiled but pulled it back. "I'm sorry. I've been on edge for so long, and now I feel lighter...free."

"There might be financial paybacks to the law enforcement departments that spent so much time trying to find her," Helen said. "He felt that we're on uneven ground and should proceed carefully. He suggested Dani telephone all concerned and then take a step back. In the meantime, he'll look into the possible repercussions, financial reimbursements if necessary."

So they were back to square one. If he told the Rimons he'd found their daughter, her life would be interrupted again. If he didn't, he couldn't accept any of their money. Beyond that, he realized it would only be a matter of time before another investigator came along, found the same lead Vaughn had, and ultimately found her again.

Vaughn saved them all. "Tony, what if Dani called from your cell phone? She could let her parents know she is alive and well and not wanting to be found. At least if the call was traced, it would go back to your number."

"If they pushed, they could probably find out the general area the call was placed from, but under the circumstances, it's the best I can do," he said.

"No matter what happens, we'll be together." Helen gave Dani's hand a quick squeeze before standing tall.

He pulled out the phone and made the call. Mrs. Rimon answered and went breathless when Tony identified himself. "Is Mr. Rimon home? Can he get on an extension so I could talk to you both?" When he had them both on the line, he handed the phone to Dani.

She took it with a shaking hand. "Momma, Daddy, it's Dani. I mean Danielle. Please don't be upset…"

Tony winced. What had her life been like back then? He knew the pressures of growing up in a family that accepted and nourished his dreams. He didn't want to think about trying to live up to his parents' expectations if they had tunnel vision.

"Momma, please don't cry. Just take a breath. I know I've disappointed you. Daddy, I'm fine, really." A look of horror crossed her face. "*No*, Dad. I don't want you to come and get me. If I wanted to be home, I wouldn't have left. If you pressure me now, you'll never find me again. Is that what you want? Because I truly mean it. I'll disappear, and nobody will ever find me."

Helen stood frozen, her hands clasped around Dani's waist.

Tony heard the explosion of voices coming from the telephone. Dani winced, holding the phone from her ear, and Helen moved her arm around her shoulders. "Mom, Dad, I'm going to hang up if you don't stop and listen to me. I'm very happy with my life now and with...Helen. Please think about it before you make any decisions that might hurt us all in the future."

Vaughn nudged Tony into the hallway, away from the conversation. She reached up and slid her hands around his neck, pulling him down to meet her lips.

"You did a good thing, Anthony Lombardo the Fifth." Her lips met his in a quick kiss, and she hugged him tighter.

Minutes later, Dani appeared in the hallway, the phone extended. "Do you know George's number?"

"He kept the same number, same home, and same everything. He wanted you to be able to find him if you tried."

She nodded and went back into the office. They heard a similar version of the earlier call, but this time it wasn't quite so harrowing.

Apparently, George was surprised she was alive, that she'd engineered her departure, and that she was calling him at that moment. Tony noticed she didn't tell either her parents or George where she was, only that she was safe and would call back tomorrow evening when they'd all had time for the shock to wear off. She apologized several times.

She told George that she'd initiate the paperwork for their divorce immediately so he could get married. She wanted him to be happy and apologized for all the years he wasn't.

****

Vaughn felt guilty all the way back to Manhattan for stepping in where she should have remained silent. Tony was the investigator. She was just a woman who could sympathize with Danielle on a strange parallel. She knew what it was like to give up the only identity she'd ever known. At least, Danielle and Helen had each other. She started to apologize once they were on the major road. Tony dismissed it, but he was quiet, making her fidgety.

"Tony?"

"The thing is, Vaughn, I can understand how you'd sympathize with her. But a note, a card, anything that would have said she was alive and wanted to be left alone. I don't get that."

"I don't either, but I can understand being desperate to survive and wanting to have some small semblance of you left intact. That doesn't change the fact that I shouldn't have interfered."

"In a way, I'm glad you did. It took the decision off my shoulders." He glanced with a half smile.

She knew they were all right. They'd come through the other side of this situation as a couple. That was a feeling she never wanted to take for granted or forget.

"Take me home, and take me to bed. It's been a long, strange day, and I want to hold you." She flashed him a quick, devilish grin. "Among other things." She turned away from him to stare out the side window, wishing they were already home.

Chapter Eleven

Guilt once again flooded through Vaughn's mind on the drive home from Brooklyn the following Tuesday. She'd met Tony's family over supper. The neighborhood—with its matching brick houses, each with a single driveway and the small patch of front and rear lawn—reminded her of home.

He showed her up the front stairs and into a living room that ran into the dining room that led into the kitchen.

"The staircase running along the far wall leads up to three bedrooms and two baths," he told her. "Half of the lower level is utility area, and the other half is den."

She could visualize the space as it once might have been, littered with Tony's and Carmen's toys and schoolbooks. His father was an older, grayer version of her Tony. His mother, Josephine, bustled around the kitchen with practiced ease, her once-dark hair now a graceful gray.

Carmen looked like her mother must have twenty-five years earlier. Her husband, Anthony, was on duty this night, but their children gathered around the table, dropping bits of food and talking over each other's tale of their school day. It was loud and confusing, and Vaughn hadn't had so much fun in years. This was what she'd been missing all these years, her family.

Her household had been different—the volume

much lower—but she remembered them having fun and laughing and smiling. She remembered how easy it was to be hugged and how she'd enjoyed the contact. Tonight when Carmen put on her children's jackets, her youngest, Cecelia, had wrapped her arms around Vaughn's legs and tried to all but climb up her.

She picked up the child and was rewarded with a wet kiss on the lips and extensive questions about when she'd come back to see her dollies. She told little Cecelia it would be her Uncle Tony she had to talk to, and she was dismissed in a heartbeat.

He walked Carmen and the kids home, leaving her to finish in the kitchen with his parents. They were kind and open with her, easily sharing a few stories of Tony's antics growing up.

"Ask him about the infamous firecracker episode entailing the decapitation of Carmen's doll collection," Josephine said later when he returned.

With a laugh, he rolled his eyes. Vaughn laughed openly and was comfortable, but her conscience bothered her when she had to hedge or outright lie about her past.

Generalities were fine. Her parents were retired in the western part of the US, and she spoke to them weekly. Her job with the radio station was safe territory as well as her voice-over work. There had been a moment over supper when she thought she wanted to die, but Josephine had soothed it over. Little Ceil had noticed the scar on her right wrist and asked how she got hurt.

Vaughn felt the color fade from her face, but Josephine came to her rescue. "Cecelia," she said enthusiastically, showing the child a scar on her forearm, "Do you know how I got this one?"

Absorbed by her grandmother's words, the child forgot about Vaughn's scar. It didn't, however, explain it to the Lombardos. That was the major thing bothering her tonight. She'd wanted to be open and honest with them, to tell them who their son had brought home. She couldn't, not completely anyway. It had bothered her to lie to people she was fond of. Lying had also put Tony in an awkward position with them.

"What's wrong, Vaughn? You're too quiet." Tony turned down the radio. "Was it too much with Carmen and the kids?"

"No, Tony. Believe it or not, kids don't bother me. Of course, on a steady diet I might change my mind, but they're smart and funny and inquisitive." She let out a deep sigh, one she'd been holding back since they got in the SUV to come home. "I feel bad because I like your parents and I didn't like lying to them. That's always going to be a problem, isn't it? I'll never be able to be honest and open with them, and that doesn't seem very fair to them. I don't want you to distance yourself from them because of me."

"I'm a forty-five-year-old retired bachelor. I've made my choices. I don't see why I can't have you and them. So please think this through before you dismiss us altogether because of your past."

She would, long and hard for days.

****

Tony noticed a visible change in Vaughn's attitude toward him in the two weeks since she'd met his family. She'd withdrawn from him, and nothing he did or said made the distance between them any better. He knew his mother had received a lovely thank-you note for the supper, and while his parents hadn't come right out and asked, they had questions about her too. He wasn't sorry he'd talked to them about her weeks before, but he didn't tell Vaughn they had any inkling that she might have something to do with the protection program.

He also knew the level of intimacy they'd once shared was withering. He was thankful he had a good reason to call her and make a date for lunch.

She was polite and controlled when she met him, refusing a heavy lunch in favor of soup. She drank only mineral water, and he knew he'd lost her. Not from her menu choices, but from the sadness that was back in her eyes. He handed her the letter from Helen and Dani.

She read it carefully.

Helen wrote:

We went to Philadelphia and met with her parents and with George. We've hired a lawyer to handle the divorce and any other problems that might come from her resurfacing. We made it clear our lives are in New York now, and we hoped in time the Rimons would come to understand and accept their daughter's choices.

Dani's handwriting added:

If they don't, they know the consequences. I've survived without them. They brought me up in a controlled environment, but they never figured I'd take control one day. I figure they never dreamed it would come back to bite them in the butt someday.

The women thanked Tony and Vaughn for allowing them to make the first step.

"I owe you a lot, Vaughn. If I'd been alone, I might have handled the situation differently," Tony said.

"I figured you'd do the right thing when the time came. I'm really proud of you. Whatever happens to them now, they'll start with a clear conscience."

"What about you, angel? Are you pushing me away because you think lying to my family is a problem? Everyone is allowed to have a past. It's our present and the future I'm thinking of, and I see my future with you."

He hadn't expected her to burst into tears and run from the restaurant. It took him a few minutes to drop money on the table and gather his jacket and her shopping bag. He caught up with her a half block later, drying her tears. He didn't ask, just walked beside her, his arm protectively around her shoulders.

When they reached the apartment building, Gus took one look at Vaughn and put on his professional face. He nodded to them both and held the door but stayed outside instead of following them into the lobby to converse. Tony knew better than to head for the elevator. She started to smile when they reached the second-floor landing, and he noticed she sped through it too. They reached the third floor, where she finally slowed and took a breath.

"What is that awful smell on two?" she asked him, the silence finally broken.

"I don't know. It always reminds me of funerals, though." His hand went to the back of her neck, a gesture familiar to both of them. "I miss you, Vaughn, and I want us back the way we used to be."

On the fourth-floor landing, she stopped to catch her breath again. For almost four months now, she'd been climbing them several times a day. Going down wasn't bad, but the fourth floor up always made her pause for air, something Tony was grateful for. It wouldn't do for her to see him lagging behind her. They wandered down the hallway and headed for her apartment.

"Have supper with me tonight. You don't have to work. We'll stay in or go out, whatever you're in the mood for."

His posture and stance changed as he moved Vaughn behind him. He'd seen the keypad to her alarm hanging from its wires. The connection had been broken. When she was safely away, he dropped the shopping bag and reached to his ankle to pull out a small pistol. He reached inside his coat and handed her his cell phone.

"Call Daniels and tell him to get over here, and don't follow me down the hallway." He tried to school his expression, but she looked past him to see what was wrong. She nodded, and his face softened. "Is there any chance I could talk you into waiting downstairs or at my place until I see what's going on in here?"

Her simple "no" was taken for fact.

"All right, but wait here and call Daniels. Don't come in until I tell you it's clear." He dropped a kiss on her forehead. Then he walked the length of the hallway and slowly pushed the door to the apartment open. The molding had been hacked away and the deadbolts pried from the doorjamb.

"Police!" he hollered from years of practice before taking a stance and a deep breath. He took a hesitant step into the apartment and stopped. The place had been ransacked.

The closet in the hallway was open, the clothing ripped from its hangers, and some of it torn. The living room was a disaster area. Books had been torn from the shelves, and crystal and china accents smashed. Her couch and chairs had been sliced open, the stuffing still floating in small bits through the air. The fireplace poker was stabbed into the corner of her reading chair by the fireplace. Tony assumed it was also used to make the deep gouges in the wall. A glance in the kitchen confirmed it had undergone the same kind of assault.

He hurried back to the hallway and told Vaughn to wait, reminding her not to come in yet, and she gave him an exaggerated frown. He didn't want to leave her alone in the hallway, but he had to make sure the apartment was empty.

He threaded his way through the debris that had once been her belongings and nudged open the french door to her bedroom. Odd. She always kept them open. One glance around the bedroom, and even he was horrified. Her clothes were dumped in piles, some of them torn. All her underclothes had been dumped around the bed, and the dresser drawers tossed haphazardly around. He also knew the wet stains on the center of her bed weren't going to turn out to be water or urine. His only hope was they'd be able to get DNA from them and someday use it to put the bastard who did this away.

The bathroom was intact, except for a large bath towel draped over the shower. The tile walls were wet, and he guessed the madman who had ransacked Vaughn's apartment had showered there. He turned around and saw the message on her mirror, written in one of her red lipsticks.

I've found you. There's nowhere for you to hide.

He wanted to go with his first instinct and wipe it away, but he knew he couldn't. He backed out of the mess and headed to the hallway, catching her just as she was about to enter.

"Out!" He grabbed the phone from her.

Gus was upstairs seconds later, out of breath and panting. He stood beside Vaughn while Tony grilled him about anyone being in the building this morning.

She had slipped away while Tony was trying to get control of his emotions and Gus was telling him he hadn't seen anybody out of the ordinary. Her scream stopped their intense discussion.

He found her in the center of her living room, turning slowly in circles to see what had been done to her home. He picked his way through the litter, and for the first time in weeks, she let him hold her close.

"My God, Tony, who hates me this much?"

Gus stood in the hallway, his face ghostly white. "Ms. Matthews, I'm so sorry. Nobody came past me this morning. It's been a quiet day, all day."

"Gus, would you go down and wait for Mr. Daniels?" Tony said. "You know who he is by now."

Gus nodded and backed out of the space, obviously glad to be away from the carnage.

"Come over to my place," Tony whispered and moved along with her as he took her across the hall. After wedging open his door, he walked her to the couch and then went back and hovered in the doorway. He kept looking from Vaughn to the hallway, waiting for Daniels and his team to arrive.

He knew Daniels from the way he moved and the light blond hair. He hit the top of the stairs with his gun drawn and was beside Tony seconds later. He pushed past him and did a visual check of Vaughn.

"Stay here," he grunted, following Tony back to her apartment.

****

Vaughn sat for a long while, her hands folded in her lap, just as they'd told her, until something inside her started to churn and boil. Wasn't it enough she'd given up years of her life? Now somebody wanted more. Why her? And why now? She walked into the hallway and followed their voices.

They stood in her bathroom, discussing the note on the mirror. The steam from the shower had left drips in the lipstick, its presentation looking like something out of an old horror movie. She held back the scream that worked through her, and both men turned to see her.

"Get out of here," Daniels hollered before composing his tone. "Don't touch anything."

His anger threw her into a tantrum she couldn't hold back any longer. "Fuck you, Daniels. It's my home and my stuff and…"

Words failed her as she realized what the madman had done on her bed with her underclothes. She bolted from the apartment, glad to be away from it. Tony found her in his bathroom a minute later, washing her face with cold water. He only opened his arms. There was no hesitation. She went willingly, her only question being "Why?"

****

Hours later, when the crime scene unit left, Vaughn was finally allowed to return to her apartment. That was how she saw it now—just an apartment, not home anymore. She was able to detach herself from the emotional side of the situation and deal with the reality of it. She'd been plied with endless cups of coffee and paced Tony's apartment for hours as a second group of strangers sorted through her clothes, her personal life...her life, such as it was left.

Just when she'd begun to let herself have one again, it seemed someone was hell-bent on taking it away from her. She stood in the doorway of her teal-and-buttercup kitchen and saw only appliances and tile grout that was hard to keep clean. The broken dishes that were so lovingly picked out became just that, dishes.

She wandered around the battered room. She watched Tony and Daniels watching her and finally broke the tension. They seemed ready for her to go to pieces again. She'd be damned if it was going to be about stuff that could be replaced.

"My financial records, are they missing?" She wanted to know the answer and wanted them to see she had pulled herself together. "They were in the bottom drawer of the desk."

Daniels pointed to a small paper bag on top of the fireplace hearth. She nodded. "Can someone at the office handle the paperwork of closing the accounts?" In actuality, she'd thought to do it earlier while she was waiting but couldn't find the strength to make the calls. Now she wished she had. It would have been something constructive instead of pacing and feeling sorry for herself. That was gone now. She was just angry for the lost time she'd never get back and the intrusion into the new life she was building.

With a practiced eye, she looked around the room. The shelf holding the dozen or so old vinyl albums didn't look disturbed. She noted the powder on the albums and the player beside them. Moving away, she stopped dead. "This isn't the album I left on."

"Are you sure?" Daniels asked.

She caught his eye roll and stormed toward him, her hands fisted at her sides. He blinked first, and she turned back to the player. "Yes, I'm sure. I was listening to the soundtrack from an old musical. This is the Duke Ellington album Tony gave me for Valentine's Day."

Whoever had broken into the apartment had known about her relationship with Tony. She and Tony looked at Daniels.

"Don't go there, either of you. I can account for my time all day. Vaughn, what time did you leave this morning?"

She told him she'd come home from work and napped for a few hours. She showered and dressed and headed out to meet Tony for lunch. She'd stopped at the bookstore and met Tony afterward at one o'clock.

"I've been in classes all morning," Tony told them with a relieved breath. "I left before nine for my lecture, and I went straight to the restaurant after. Gus will confirm I didn't come back."

"Well, assuming I couldn't do this—" She laughed aloud. Both men watched her but didn't join in. "Well, really, the stains." She laughed again. Neither man did. They apparently assumed she was holding on by a thread but weren't sure how to handle her.

"I can get Jacob on the phone for you, Vaughn. Would that help?" Tony offered.

"No, don't bother him. I'll call him tomorrow when we know more about what's going on. There's no sense getting him upset with unknowns."

She reached down to pick up a green ceramic flowerpot. She'd never gotten around to buying a plant to put in it. Tony was watching her intently when Daniels's cell phone rang. He moved to her and pulled her into the hallway.

"I'd like to take you to Brooklyn for the night. Will you come with me?"

She studied his face, his eyes. She stroked his jaw, the stubble a welcome texture against her fingers. "Yes, but only because you asked and didn't order me." She stood up on tiptoes and kissed him lightly. "I miss you, Tony, but I'm so afraid, for so many obvious reasons."

Holding her to his body, he whispered, "I promise we'll figure it out, angel. Let's go get Daniels out of there, and we'll blow this joint."

His Humphrey Bogart accent was horrible, but she appreciated him trying and managed a half smile.

Pausing in the once-secure doorway, she remembered how careful she was to lock and alarm it each time she came and went. She glanced at Daniels. "I suppose I shouldn't worry about anybody breaking in while I'm gone. What's left to take?" It was a resigned voice, not an angry one.

"I've got a man on the way over. He'll watch the door tonight and stay until the team comes over tomorrow to replace the door and the alarm. I can have it cleaned up if you want, Vaughn."

"No, thanks. I'll come back tomorrow and pick through, see if anything is salvageable."

"Let's worry about that tomorrow. For now, if you need her, call her cell. I'm taking her away for the night." Tony moved his hand to her shoulder.

Vaughn pulled from him, stopping in the living

room doorway. With one last look, she let him lead her away.

Chapter Twelve

Vaughn hesitated at the top of the stairs, and Tony reached for her hand. She shook her head and started back to her apartment. Close behind her, he followed her back. She took off her coat and folded it neatly, dropped her purse on the floor and the coat on top of it outside her doorway.

"It's better if I face it now."

She didn't wait for him to answer, and in an odd way he knew what she meant.

Daniels seemed surprised to see them back and hung up his phone. "What did you forget?" He watched her push back her sleeves.

Tony only raised one of his eyebrows in answer to his same unasked question.

"I saw that." She palmed his butt as she walked past him toward the kitchen.

"I don't think she'll leave until she's taken back some control," he told Daniels.

"You're right," she said, returning from the kitchen.

Tony moved back to the hallway and hollered that he was taking her coat and purse. She followed him into his apartment and watched him drop them on the sofa.

"I'll make a pot of coffee," he said. He returned quickly with a box of garbage bags and handed them to her. "I'll be over in a few minutes."

She left, and when he returned to her apartment, she was sweeping up debris while Daniels made an inventory of the items she rattled off.

"The china was a service for eight. The charge will be on my credit card. The glasses and mugs were all bought at the same time. The flatware seems to all be here." She gave him the name of the store.

"Count them anyway," Tony said. "Coffee's brewing and should be ready in five minutes." He tugged a bag from the box and took the full one from the pail she'd been filling with debris. He moved the dustpan closer and held it in place while she swept pieces of blue-and-yellow dinner plates onto it. Daniels counted her flatware. The service for eight accounted for.

Vaughn quickly opened the dishwasher door, pulled out the bottom rack, and set the offending utensils in it. "The carving knife is gone."

"We found it," Daniels said with a discontented grunt.

"Where?" Her tone was just as caustic.

"Doesn't matter. It's accounted for," he countered.

She shot him a dirty look over her shoulder. "Don't treat me like a child, Chester Daniels."

Tony couldn't hold back a snort of laughter. "*Chester*? No wonder all your records just say C. Daniels. Ch…" He turned away. "The coffee should be ready," he said as he left the room. He knew they could hear him muttering "Chester" several times before he was out of their hearing range.

****

"Low blow, Vaughn." Daniels looked wounded, and a pout formed on his lips as his eyes narrowed.

"Yes, I agree. Childish, actually, just the way you've been treating me. Now, where did you find my carving knife?"

His temper slipped out in his tone, his words clipped. "It was stuffed between the mattress and the box spring. If you'd lain on the bed, it would have probably punctured you. Happy now? This guy is crazy, and you need to leave for a while. Just take a vacation. Go anywhere for a few weeks, back to Seattle to see Jacob. Hell, go to Europe. I don't care. Just don't stay here right now."

She opened the cabinet doors. Her pots and pans were intact, but she threw them all in the dishwasher. The dish towels and the rest of the kitchen appeared intact. She quickly washed and dried the sink and countertops, wearing bright pink rubber gloves. When that task was done, she took the newest towel from the bottom of the pile to dry her hands. She gathered the whole drawer full and dropped them into a clean plastic bag.

"More laundry." She sighed. That was the least of her worries.

With the floor swept, the room didn't look like quite such a disaster area. She grabbed another garbage bag and moved to the refrigerator. She used the hand towel to prop open the freezer door and flung the ice trays in the sink. She unceremoniously dumped all the food into the garbage. She pulled out a few plastic containers of stew and spaghetti sauce she'd made and tossed them too. She did the same with everything in the refrigerator; only the cans of soda didn't get pitched.

"Such a waste of time, energy, and food. Did the

lab take any of it to be tested?" she asked Daniels.

He was back in a chair at her kitchen table, still annoyed. He'd been keeping up a running list of the things she was throwing out.

She looked at him to see if he was listening to her. "I don't expect the insurance company to pay for my groceries too. I just don't want to take a chance."

Tony returned with a thermos of coffee and three coffee mugs looped around his finger.

"We're just about done here in the kitchen. Can we take that in the living room?" She pushed past him, not waiting for an answer.

"Sure, unless you want to take a break," he said, following her.

"No, let's just get this cleanup over with as soon as possible." She tried to hold back her sigh but didn't quite manage.

****

They moved to the living room, and Tony handed around mugs of the steaming brew. Daniels turned to a clean page on his legal pad and started listing the furniture that had been torn to shreds. Vaughn gathered bits of debris and rattled off what the item had once been and where she'd gotten it and how much it cost. It went that way for the next half hour. Tony collected garbage, and Daniels made lists. No doubt she was saying goodbye to the few precious possessions she'd begun to collect.

"The worst is yet to come, boys. You two up for it?" Her false bravado didn't fool him.

She left them abruptly and returned wearing her pink rubber gloves again. She handed a second pair to Tony, yellow and obviously larger. "Think these will fit?" she asked, as if it were just another day and another task to get through.

He didn't question her mood. She held the garbage bag open this time while he pulled the bed skirt from the box spring. The mattress stood on its side, leaning against the far wall, its soiled layers of bedding taken to the lab. A neat square of the mattress had been cut out for laboratory testing. He didn't miss her body shudder as she realized that was where the knife was found.

She glanced at Tony and went back to the piles of clothing. She made quick work of realizing each article had been abused one way or another. The piles of her underclothes were worse. He was proud of how she was handling the situation. Get it done and get it over with. He figured she was doing a mental inventory.

She paused when she noticed both men were watching her. "Tony, the only thing missing that I can see right now is the pink set."

He acknowledged her words with a nod, not expanding on the significance of the missing items. Daniels leaned against the bathroom doorframe and waited for one of them to fill him in.

Finally, Vaughn spoke, but not before turning her back to Daniels. "The matching bra-and-panty set, pink. It's missing."

"No chance it's at the laundry?" Daniels asked, his tone clipped.

"No. I hand-wash my underclothes."

"Why the pink set, Vaughn? What's the significance?" This time he didn't try to hide his attitude.

"It's the set I was wearing the first night Tony and I…"

"I get it, but how would anybody know?"

Tony assumed he didn't expect an answer to his rhetorical question.

"It means I've been watched more than I...we realized, doesn't it? It means someone has been watching me, outside the apartment. It means he knew I stayed at Tony's that night. It's the only answer." She sat on the bedroom floor. She didn't say anything else. She simply let her legs fold under her.

"Could he have gotten the information from a credit slip?" Daniels offered, and Tony figured he was probably trying to take the pressure off her.

"Yes, but I doubt it, and so do you. Tony, what do you think?"

"I think we have to get a camera set up at the back entrance," he said, and in a stage whisper added, "I can't believe there isn't one there already." He took several deep, cleansing breaths. "We're going to set one up in the hallway too."

Vaughn looked at Daniels. "You said the apartments across the street had been checked. Was that true?"

"Yes, they were all vetted months ago, before you leased this apartment. I'll have the occupants screened again."

"And their window treatments checked," Tony added.

"I agree with all these items," Daniels said, "especially the cameras at the rear entrance, one in the hallway, and one on the staircase railing. I'll make the calls. The alarm team can set it up tomorrow." His phone rang, and after a short conversation, he turned back to Vaughn and Tony. "The team is downstairs.

They checked the rear lock. It was trashed, but it must have been done sometime last night. Gus would have heard the noise if it happened today. No weapon was found in the alley, and none of the neighbors directly below were home today." He left quickly, his ever-present cell phone in hand.

Tony moved beside Vaughn and extended his hand. "Time to get out of here."

Smiling, she let him help her to her feet. "I agree. Just let me clean out the bathroom. This way when I come back, it will all be done."

They went to her once-pristine bathroom and ignored the writing on the mirror. She dumped all the cosmetics and toiletries into a bag Tony held open. When the room was bare, she tossed in the throw rug and hand towels that had been hanging. The rest of her linens looked untouched, but he knew she'd have them laundered before using them again. She slowly turned in the space she had once been so comfortable in. He understood that feeling was gone for her.

"Come on. It's time to go. There's nothing more you can do here tonight," he said.

"The mirror." She paused to look at his face.

"Let Chester get it," he teased.

She honored him with a small smile. "All right."

Daniels was talking to a younger man. After briefly introducing herself, Vaughn apologized for the lack of food in the apartment. She told them to help themselves to the sodas she'd left. Both men dutifully thanked her and dismissed her with a nod.

Tony paused beside Daniels. "Thanks for your help tonight. Can we get together tomorrow to talk this over?"

"Call me in the morning, and we'll put something together."

"Use her cell phone if you need us." Tony led Vaughn back to his apartment. He gathered her coat and purse, grabbed his jacket, and walked her to the elevator.

"You just don't want to have to deal with the smell on two," she told him.

He knew she was trying to lighten their moods. He slipped his arm around her to pull her close and pressed his lips to her forehead. No words could comfort her. She knew too much already. His truck waited for them at the entrance, and she let him fold her into the front seat and adjust the belt across her, glancing around.

"I didn't realize how late it was."

"You must be hungry?" he said.

"Not really."

"Well, you better find an appetite before we get to Brooklyn, or you'll find yourself being force-fed."

She quietly watched the traffic flow around them as he voice activated the phone. She closed her eyes and rested her head against the car window.

"Hi, Mom."

"Tony, it's late. Is everything okay?"

"No, nothing drastic is wrong. I'm bringing Vaughn home for the night. Her apartment was…vandalized."

****

Vaughn cringed at the term but knew any other he used would have been worse.

"Is Carmen over with the kids?"

The rest of their conversation went past her unheard. In her mind, all she wanted to know was who hated her this much. Somehow it didn't seem right to blame this all on Reno. But if not, who else? It was too much to try to figure out. Her mind was fatigued, to say the least.

She let herself fall asleep, away from the horrible image her mind conjured of the knife sticking up from under her mattress.

She roused from her escape sleep. It was close to midnight when Tony parked in his parents' driveway. Although the day had warmed, the cold evening air that greeted her outside the heated truck shocked her lungs, burning with each breath she took.

The light was on over the front door, the living room light filtering through first a layer of heavy drapes pulled against the night, then a pair of white sheer curtains. The slice of light that shone through was oddly comforting. They hadn't reached the top step when Tony's mother pulled open the inside door for them.

"Come in. It's cold. You'll catch a chill." She took Vaughn from Tony's arm, helping her off with her coat and handing it to Tony. She efficiently escorted her upstairs to the bathroom and told her to freshen up and join them in the kitchen.

Vaughn was grateful for the time alone. Still half-asleep and half-traumatized from the afternoon, she washed her face, appreciating the soft, clean towel that awaited her. The brush in her purse made some semblance of order in her brunette hair, the overhead light glinting on her red highlights.

Not so long ago she would have smiled at the natural color and highlights. This time when she disappeared into obscurity, she'd go back to being a blonde. She'd only been kidding herself these last months. She'd never be normal, never have an average life. She had to accept the inevitable and make a new plan and in time, implement it somewhere far away from New York City. Unfortunately, she knew she couldn't stay here now. Her draw to Tony was too intense, and he was too important to let anyone hurt him or his family.

That was how he found her, just leaving the bathroom. "Better? Mom's got some sandwich stuff laid out. Let's get something to eat."

She nodded. To refuse would be pointless. She was hungry, and Mrs. Lombardo had already gone to the trouble. Vaughn took his outstretched hand but halted outside the middle bedroom. She stood in the doorway, then ran her hand along the wall, feeling for the light switch.

When she hit it, the room glowed around her. It was quite a revelation. Tony had grown up here, in this space. She wanted to know what it was like. The walls were navy blue, but all the trim and the ceiling white. Matching dark blue and red plaid curtains mimicked the bedspread. Dark wood dressers and a desk completed the room.

"It was never this clean when I lived here," he told her.

She laughed at the idea. For years she and her mother had fought over the right for her to have her private space, territory that was meant for no one else to see, especially parents.

Her messy years hadn't lasted long. She was more of a pack rat, wanting to keep a token from each of her memories. Her mirror was filled with snapshots of friends in stupid poses. Movie and concert ticket stubs were taped around the frame. A midterm with an A ceremoniously hung in a conspicuous place, a reminder she could accomplish what she set out to do if it interested her.

The flood of memories almost overwhelmed her. She could clearly remember every poster that had graced her walls, from rock gods to Hollywood idols. It was all so teen oriented yet so perfect.

At least she was smart enough to realize it at the time and enjoy it to the degree a teenager could. How she wished sometimes she could close her eyes and go back to that time. A time when she was making choices and decisions. Maybe one small change would have made the difference in her overall life.

Closing her eyes, she shook away the idea. She was one woman who knew there was no going back, and second-guessing her history would drive her crazy if she let it.

Words Tony spoke earlier in the day came back. "I miss you, Vaughn. I want us back the way we used to be."

So did she, and that couldn't happen. She was the only one who could jump-start the changes to make it happen.

Chapter Thirteen

Tony Bennett serenaded them from the small radio on the kitchen counter. Vaughn was amazed at the food laid out on the table. Sliced ham and turkey as well as thin slices of swiss cheese sat beside fresh rye bread. Bowls of steaming lentil soup were being dished up as she slid into a seat across from Anthony Lombardo the Fourth. His smile was kind, and his eyes still clear.

"My Jo makes the best soups in Brooklyn," he told Vaughn.

Jo Lombardo blushed and tossed the dish towel at her husband. The look that crossed between them wasn't lost on Tony, who didn't hold back his smile. It was a look of love and understanding that came with years of devotion.

She watched and listened to their banter and their tales of growing up in Brooklyn. There were tales of Carmen and Tony as children with their grandparents living just a house or two away.

"Both sets of my grandparents died when I was very young, too young to remember much of any of them that hadn't been told to me with accompanying photos. How lucky Carmen and Anthony's children are to be so close to their family," she said, not adding that even if they never really understood it, she knew the difference.

She sipped at the cooling soup as the conversation

went from the impending baseball season to the tax structure and the proposed new schools. Vaughn hardly noticed when the bowl was taken from her and a clean plate put in its place. She made half a sandwich after much prompting from Jo and Anthony. She ate without thinking, enjoying the new taste of homemade pickled tomatoes.

The sandwiches cleared away, a hot mug of coffee was pressed into her hands and a slice of homemade cinnamon Danish pushed before her. She threw up her hands to defend herself from the plate of fresh apples, grapes, and chunks of cheddar cheese that replaced the cake. The dish of candied almonds was too much to resist.

She pushed her chair back from the table. She was sated like never before, only in a different way. She'd been allowed to be a part of their family for a short time, accepted without questions.

"Will you stay with us while your apartment is being fixed, Vaughn? It would be a pleasure to have someone who appreciates my cooking for a change." Jo teased her husband as he pulled her onto his lap. Her hand went around his neck, and she kissed his cheek.

"Thank you, but no. I appreciate you feeding me tonight, but I have to get back to the city tomorrow. Between work and getting the apartment back in shape, it's going to take a few weeks to find normal again." The words flowed so easily from her lips. Normal, something she'd found for a short time and knew was gone, at least at this time in her life.

"Maybe it wouldn't be such a bad idea, Vaughn," Tony said.

A veil of darkness overtook her when she

momentarily considered the offer. But she wouldn't stay here. She'd go back to prove a point, even if just to herself. "I really do appreciate you wanting me here, but traveling at night for work isn't a good idea, and there will be decisions I have to make." She shook off her dark mood. These people didn't deserve her depressive attitudes. "Besides, I have some major shopping to do in the next few days."

She teased easily with a bright smile. The problem was it was just a little too bright, and the three other people at the table apparently realized it because they averted their gazes.

"Well, for tonight, we'll put you in Carmen's old room," Jo said.

"That's fine. I will have to be up early," Vaughn reiterated. She knew there was no way in hell Tony was going to allow her to jump on a train or subway to get back to Manhattan tomorrow before he ever opened his mouth to say the words.

"I'll drive you back whenever you're ready in the morning." His tone warned it was a statement not to be toyed with or questioned.

She nodded but didn't let it drop. "What time does rush hour start? What time can you be ready to head out?"

Judging by the expressions on the faces of the people sitting around the table, especially Tony's, they all understood the conversation was going nowhere near where Tony would have liked. He deferred by telling her whenever she was awake and ready in the morning, he'd take her home. Jo showed her back upstairs to the second small bedroom. She pulled open two drawers in the chest.

"Use anything that's comfortable, Vaughn. These are some of Carmen's things she stored here after little Ceil was born. Her thin clothes, as she called them. I doubt she even remembers they're still here."

She hated that Jo Lombardo was witnessing her stable life crumble. Falling in love with Jo's son was dangerous to them all, especially this woman who she was beginning to care for. She closed the drawer and walked the last few steps to the bed. Sitting beside her, she moved her arm around Vaughn's shoulders.

Vaughn accepted the warm embrace, grateful for a female who might sympathize with how she was feeling. While she didn't cry in great sobs, a few tears strayed down her cheeks.

Jo took a clean tissue from her apron pocket and handed it to her. "It will all work out in the end. You just have to work your way through it," she whispered.

Vaughn finally inched away, embarrassed by her show of emotion to an almost total stranger. Where was her resolve to make it alone? Where was the strength she'd fought so hard to find in the last two years? Her resolve seemed to be deserting her when she needed it most. It didn't help that she genuinely liked these people.

"Thank you for tonight. I couldn't have stayed there."

"Of course not, and you know the door here will always be open to you, no matter what happens, Tony or not. Do you understand?"

She couldn't find words to answer. Instead, she twisted the tissue between her fingers.

"Sleep well. If you need anything, Tony's next door, and Anthony and I are at the head of the hall."

"Thank you, I'll be fine. I just need a few hours' sleep."

"Nobody will bother you here tonight. Lie back and close your eyes. You're safe to sleep." Jo turned on the small bedside light and shut off the overhead. "Pleasant dreams." She left the door ajar behind her.

The sound of Anthony's and Tony's voices filtering up the stairs comforted her. She wasn't alone.

****

Downstairs, Jo, Anthony, and Tony finished cleaning up the mess from their late meal. They sat over a small glass of anisette, quiet in the early-morning darkness.

"Thanks for tonight, Mom. I wanted to get her out of there for a few hours."

"You did the right thing, son. Do you have any idea who broke into her apartment?" His father's voice was low.

His father's police training had kicked in. Light came back into his face. All those years of experience had been put on a shelf when he retired.

"It's complicated, Dad. I can't go into much. Possibly a stalker from her past or maybe a new one. We're not sure. The marshal in charge of her case is doing some digging."

His mother caught his slip. "Marshal, Tony? They oversee the witness program. You saw him at the federal building. You were right."

"You found your ten percent of the missing puzzle," Anthony added.

"No, only about one percent. There's still some crazy out there. He's the last bit of the puzzle." Jo sat back and smiled at her son.

He shot his mother a look that told her she was right, but he wasn't going to confirm or deny anything. Yawning, he stood and pushed his chair under the table. "Goodnight, Dad. Mom, thanks for supper on such short notice."

"Night, Tony." his mother answered as he leaned down to kiss her cheek.

"Sometimes you're too smart for your own good," he whispered. They laughed at his final acknowledgment on the subject. "Night."

"If you can talk her into staying here, we'll make her as comfortable as possible. With your sister's husband only a house away and me here, she should be safe."

"Thanks, Dad. I know, but I think she's afraid of putting you in harm's way. I'll see what I can talk her into tomorrow."

"Go up and check on her. Make sure she's asleep," his mother told him.

He left his parents in an all-too-familiar spot. They sat next to each other at the kitchen table, only the small stove light on, a glass or cup in front of each of them, their hands lightly folded together between them on the surface. The only thing missing was the big glass ashtray that used to sit in the center of the table, as well as the ever-present pack of cigarettes and the silver lighter that was never supposed to leave the kitchen.

They had both quit cold turkey when his dad retired. He never knew how they'd done it and managed to stay married. They hadn't used patches or gum—just their resolve.

He smiled to himself as he took the stairs two at a time, thankful he still had them both in his life.

****

Vaughn stood at the window overlooking the back of the house. A road separated the rows of houses, then someone's backyard, and their house. The pattern repeated to the corner. All planned out in neat rows, for neat lives. Tony stood in the doorway of his sister's old bedroom, watching her.

"I couldn't sleep," she said without turning around.

"Your body probably thinks it's Thursday and you should be at work."

"I don't know where I belong, Tony. It seems like there's no place to go anymore that I'm not being hunted. I really thought I could hide in plain sight and get away with it. Now I know it will never really be over." She heard only resentment in her voice and hated the defeat she was accepting.

"Daniels is working on it, checking on Reno and if he has any reach. I'll see what I can find out. It will end, angel. I promise." He moved into the room and stood behind her, his hands on her shoulders.

She let him take her weight, her head resting on his shoulder. "Thanks for taking me away tonight. But we both know I can't stay here. It's not safe for your parents or your sister and her family. Please explain that to them, because I wouldn't want them to think I'm ungrateful."

"Will you stay with me until your apartment is repainted?"

Her hand slipped over his, tightening before she answered. "Thanks, but no. I've decided to go to a hotel for a few weeks. It will take a while to get the place ready, and it will give me some space from it. Hopefully, by the time it's finished, I'll be ready to go back."

"Want some company at that hotel with room service and laundry service? Anything this old man could provide in the way of services that might ease your transition?" His teasing lightened her mood.

"I'll let you know if I come up with anything."

For a long time, they stood that way with Vaughn pressed against him, her hand locked with his resting on her shoulder, the unknown between them. With a sigh, she moved away.

"I'm going to lie down for a while." She let her weight drop onto the mattress and finally let her head find the waiting pillow.

He pulled off her boots and swung her legs up onto the bed. He draped the bedspread over her shoulders before he settled in the rocking chair in the corner. He dozed lightly while she slept. It was his responsibility to keep her safe.

****

Tony woke with a start. Morning light filtered through the curtains. The bedspread had been draped over his aching body in the rocker. He tossed the blanket aside and stood, rubbing the sleep from his eyes. Vaughn was long gone from the bed, her pillow cold to his touch. Panic welled inside him, and he only hoped he hadn't slept through her leaving. When he was about to bolt down the stairs to find out, her voice filtered up through the stairwell along with the smell of fresh coffee being brewed. He paused long enough to use the bathroom and to splash some water on his face.

Standing before the mirror, he wondered who the man looking back was. All he knew was that this man was rapidly losing the woman he'd fallen in love with to circumstances out of his control. The only way he'd have any chance of having a life with Vaughn was to find out who was chasing her. He'd get what information he could out of Daniels. He laughed aloud as he remembered her calling him Chester. He carried the smile as he entered the kitchen, where a familiar sight of family overwhelmed him. Seeing Vaughn with them completed the picture. She sat with a mug of coffee cooling in front of her, a section of the newspaper in her hands. Beside her, his father sat in a similar position. His mother was at the stove, the bacon she was frying making his empty stomach rumble.

He pulled a mug from the cabinet and dropped a wet kiss on her cheek. She shooed him away, and he sat heavily onto the empty seat beside Vaughn. He glanced at the clock over the kitchen doorway. It was just past six. Breakfast went quickly, and he wasn't surprised to hear Vaughn had walked with his father to get the fresh bagels and bialys they ate.

Their drive back to Manhattan was uneventful, the roadways filling with every mile of road they crossed. When they reached the city, he parked the SUV in its outrageously expensive garage a block away from his apartment. He dropped his arm on her shoulders as they walked to the building.

"Come home with me. We'll shower, and you can decide how you want to spend your day." It was a peace offering. He was trying to give her some space as well as stay in the picture.

"Yes, to the shower, but I've got a lot to do today. Shopping being the first one that comes to mind. I've got to pick up a few essentials, and hopefully, the crew sent over will get me...the apartment secured."

He stopped the flood of excuses with a hard kiss on the lips. When he pulled away, it was only to direct her from the center of the sidewalk. His body backed her against the cold brick wall while his lips found hers again.

"Shower first. Everything else after, all right?" He hadn't wanted to stop kissing her, but his body betrayed his other morning impulses.

"Shower first," she agreed.

****

When they were back on the fourth floor, she was relieved to see several men in her apartment doorway. They were all busy as she paused by them. One pulled damaged wood from the doorjamb, while another worked with a small screwdriver in her alarm keypad. The third man looked familiar, but she couldn't place him. Was he one of the crew from last night? He didn't meet her look as she passed. Rather, he seemed determined to avoid her.

"Shower?" Tony whispered from behind.

She nodded and left with him, not caring who watched her go into his apartment. An odd feeling stayed with her all day. She couldn't shake it, but with everything that had happened in the last eighteen hours, she was allowed to be jumpy.

She showered quickly with Tony, but they didn't attempt to have sex. Instead, they used the time as an exercise in closeness. His fingers massaged her scalp and kneaded her shoulders. They managed to get through their morning routine without mentioning the rest of the day.

Tony left her to finish drying her hair and came back with a triumphant smile. He held out a pair of her white bikini panties and matching bra. Her thick white cotton socks lay on top of them. The white turtleneck sweater they lay on was hers.

She remembered pulling on his long terry robe and sneaking across the hall one morning to get dressed after their night together.

"I don't have any jeans, but when you're shopping today, buy some extras to leave here." He handed her the pile of her clothing.

She was never so thankful for clean clothes. Her original thought to put on the same things she'd worn all day yesterday and fallen asleep in wasn't comforting. Now, because Tony had done her laundry, she'd have fresh clothes to wear. She didn't acknowledge his comment about her leaving some things there.

"I didn't realize these were missing yesterday." She smiled. "And you didn't remind me either."

"I figured we gave Chester enough to think about. Where you leave your underwear should only concern you and me."

She nodded. "Thanks for doing my laundry." Subject closed.

****

Tony tried to be as undemanding as he could under the circumstances. Keeping a tight rein on Vaughn now would have been the worst mistake he could make. He told her about his afternoon meeting with Chester Daniels and couldn't keep the smile from his voice. He planned to head to the station house and see if any similar break-ins had happened around them. Her features relaxed when she heard she wasn't going to have a bodyguard.

"I've got to grab some basics, and then I'll be back here this afternoon. How about I buy you a late supper before I go to work?" Her arms slipped easily around his neck for a kiss. "By then we'll know what hotel I'll be staying in. Maybe room service?" she teased before pulling from his embrace.

"I'm game. How about we meet back here around six?"

"Great, and before you ask, yes, I have my cell phone, and it's charged."

"Be careful, okay?"

"Definitely." She left his bedroom and wandered through his living room. Her coat and purse safely retrieved, she looked back. "Thanks for last night, Tony. Brooklyn was a good idea. Please thank your parents for me."

Then she was gone from his home—and probably soon gone from his life.

Chapter Fourteen

Vaughn left Tony's and was gathering the bag with her towels and sheets from the linen closet when Daniels called.

"I found you a place to stay." His voice was blunt. He rattled off an address and told her he'd be waiting there by ten.

She dropped off her laundry and made the trip without incident. The walk in the brisk morning air revived her, renewed her. But her body was telling her she should be heading home to sleep. Today she overrode the urge to curl up someplace quiet and sleep. There was no getting around her need for some fresh clothes, and that had to take a priority. There'd be no luxury of shopping at her leisure either, choosing a shirt or sweater because she liked them or found the sale price too good to pass by. Today she'd shop because it was a necessity.

She quickly walked through the small studio space, Chester Daniels beside her. She could stay just about anywhere for a few weeks, and this would be more than adequate. It was a bright space in a residential hotel only a few blocks from her apartment. A secure building with round-the-clock doormen and a twenty-four-hour coffee shop next door. What more could she ask for?

Daniels introduced her to the daytime doorman and

handed her a set of keycards. He'd checked the grated windows, and the fire escape was at the far end of the hallway. Once she was locked in, she'd be safe. Her only problem would be when she was out of the room. She didn't expect him to alarm the place for the two or three weeks she'd be staying there. The security cameras on every floor were supposedly being monitored and recordings kept for review.

"I've used this place before. It's a good site. You'll be okay here." He walked her to the street level and didn't offer to accompany her shopping; rather, he told her to call him with any problems or if she was uncomfortable or scared. Hesitating outside the coffee shop, a cardboard cup in his hand, he blushed before her.

She couldn't believe what she was seeing and thought to tease him about it, but it would be insensitive. He'd gone out of his way to make her life easier since the day she met him. Trying to lighten the darkness that showed on his brow, she spoke first.

"Thanks for finding me a place to stay and helping me yesterday, but I'm not sorry I called you 'Chester.' " Her lips broke into a smile seconds later.

He looked as if he were deciding whether to kiss her or throttle her. He did neither, and she was grateful when he finally spoke.

"I never stood a chance, did I?" There was no need to elaborate on the topic. "Even before Lombardo. It's because I remind you of Marcus, isn't it?"

She let her gaze meet his. "Some. You're both the same height and coloring, the same clear blue eyes."

"It's all right, Vaughn. You don't have to say it. I just wondered."

"I've always been attracted to dark men. Marcus was different, and I trusted him, and he tried to kill me. It's not just your blue eyes. It's any man with blue eyes like his."

"I'm glad the bastard is dead," Daniels said.

"So am I. And I understand that's a terrible thing to think about someone you loved or thought you did, but it's true. It's something I live with every day."

"Would contacts and a dye job help?" he asked with a half smile.

"No, but thanks for the offer. Besides, I know how hard it is to be something for another person instead of for yourself. I'm used to you now, Daniels, just the way you are."

He gave her a rueful smile.

"Besides, I know your lifestyle…"

His cheeks flushed pink, and she laughed. "What I need most is a friend I can count on and trust, not a sex partner."

"Is that what Lombardo is? Just sex?"

"No, which makes this so much harder."

"I've no right to ask you. I understand you're an adult capable of making your own decisions. Just know if he hurts you in any way, I'll make him sorry." The darkness was gone from his face, acceptance and a grin replacing the frown.

"I'll let you know if it comes to that, but it won't. Besides, I didn't come to Manhattan looking for a relationship. I came for my job and to find myself and being honest, to lose myself in the vastness of all this around me." She glanced up at the tall buildings surrounding her. "Tony doesn't need my kind of trouble haunting him. With a little time, he'll get the hint and fade away too."

"You're wrong there, totally wrong if you think he'll go quietly into the night. The man's in love with you, and that's a fact. You have to decide if you love him enough to trust him."

"I do, but it doesn't matter. I'm a threat to him and his family. No, I'll slip away quietly so he won't have a choice. Like you said, I'm an adult. I make my choices. For now, at this time in my life, I need to be alone, independent."

"You keep telling yourself that and see if you believe it after a while." He bent quickly and kissed her cheek. "If you need me, I'll have the phone on."

He disappeared around the corner, leaving her to wonder just how transparent her feelings were. She took a second look around her to memorize the building and her new surroundings. She, too, walked around the corner with the intention of flagging down a cab. Instead, she walked so she could get acquainted with her new neighborhood.

****

Tony sat at the small round table in the darkened bar, a half-empty beer in front of him. He saw Daniels come in, scan the room, and head straight to him. Tony's arm came up, and the bartender saw him. By the time Daniels made his way across the room, two fresh beers waited.

"Thanks." Daniels grabbed one of the mugs and took a long pull from it before taking off his coat and dropping onto the seat beside Tony. "No prints that were usable." He pulled a small notepad from his shirt pocket and flipped through several pages. "The alarm guys will be finished by tonight, as well as the new door hung with new locks. They already have the back entrance rewired and the cameras set on motion detectors. Nobody from the building but Gus knows about it, not even the evening doorman."

"Good. That should help if this guy decides to come back. I spent some time checking on similar break-ins, but there isn't much that parallels this."

"Did you think there would be?" Daniels had pushed back in his seat, his legs extended under the empty chair beside him.

"No, but it would have taken the pressure off. Do you know who's behind this, Ches...Daniels?" They eyed each other, and Daniels appeared to accept the peace offering of sorts from Tony.

"I put in a few calls to Texas, got a few people checked out. I don't think Reno has any real power left, and Mike Elder never had that kind of clout. He was always a hired hand."

"Who took over Reno's business interests when he finally went down?"

"That would be Hal Greer. He's much smarter than Reno ever was. If anything, I'd say Vaughn did him a favor when she took Reno out of the picture, but I got somebody checking to make sure he's not interested in her." Daniels took another sip of his beer.

"What about the radio station?"

"Getting nowhere fast on that one. We started with the personnel at the station and moved to the building employees. Nothing so far that would tie in to Vaughn in any way."

"Daniels, are you really sure Marcus is dead? Could that have been a fabrication to tie up a loose end and give him a way out?"

"Don't think so, Lombardo. Jacob was still involved. He was convinced the hit was real."

"Nothing adds up. Maybe she's just got an obsessive fan?"

"Could be. None of it makes sense to me either, including you." Daniels raised his glass and finished his beer. He lowered the glass to the table with a thunk.

"I'd say as long as I make sense to Vaughn," Tony told him.

"So does she."

They sat quietly while the bartender walked another round to them. When half the liquid was gone, Daniels spoke again. "Two things and I'll drop it."

Tony waited for what was to come next. He had a few ideas but wasn't sure if he was on the right track, so he stayed silent.

"If I find out you hurt her in any way, I'll hurt you too. Make no mistake, Lombardo. I'll make you regret it."

Tony only nodded. He'd thought it was going to be something like that. "Thanks. I'll keep that in mind."

"Second, she's getting ready to cut you loose. Watch your back. She's afraid something will happen to you or your family. I'm serious. She's back to wanting to be independent and fearless again."

"She can be both and still be married to me." He didn't smile. He kept his expression dead serious. He wanted Daniels to understand he wasn't just using her.

"She know about that plan?"

"In general, yes." They laughed. "I know I deserve all the heartache I get and then some from your point of view."

"And then some." Daniels finished his beer and

stood. He pulled money from his pocket, but Tony told him it was taken care of. "Thanks for the beer. I'll keep you posted on what I find out in Texas."

"I'd appreciate that. It will keep us both from doing double time."

"She's set up in a residential hotel a few blocks from here. It's a secure spot, as secure as we can really get at this point since she refuses to leave Manhattan or accept a bodyguard."

"She needs her space right now. I appreciate you helping her."

"I was helping her, Lombardo, not you. And remember what I said—I like Vaughn, and I won't stand her being hurt."

"No problem," Tony reiterated.

Chester Daniels left quickly, his coat half on, half off, as he disappeared into the bright light of the open door. Tony sat back and thought over what he'd learned. Aside from the fact Daniels would like to take a piece of his hide for Vaughn falling for him, they were back where they started, with no clear leads.

****

Chester Daniels had been right about Vaughn starting to pull away from him. She had taken Tony to supper at the coffee shop beside her building. They'd danced around anything serious, talked about his lecture that day and her shopping excursion. After they'd picked at their burgers and fries, she had taken him to her hotel, where she'd introduced him to the evening doorman.

Inside the small studio, she waited while he checked out her new space.

"Not bad for such short notice," he said.

"A lot better than some of the places I've been temporarily stashed."

"Vaughn." He turned around in the space and found her with a strange look on her face. "What is it?" Her look told him trouble was brewing. She'd squared her shoulders and taken a stance, her body language telling him everything he needed to know without her speaking. Instead of challenging her, he backed off. "I should go. You have to get ready for work. Have lunch with me tomorrow?"

"No, thanks. I'm going to need sleep, and I'll probably crash tomorrow."

"Supper, then?"

She only shook her head.

"I'll give you some space, Vaughn. But I won't let you run me away. I'm in for the long haul, and you know it." He moved closer to the door but stopped to place a light kiss on her lips. "My family is safe no matter what you think, and I'm not disappearing to make it easier on you. If you don't want me, that's one thing, but I won't be run off by your fears. Understand?"

She gave him a scathing look, a formal challenge.

He burst out laughing—not the desired effect she was looking for, he figured. "I'm going away for a few days on business. Think about us. I'll figure out who's stalking you, and we'll take care of it. Then we'll talk about our future." His statement made, he left her standing in the center of her new apartment, apparently stunned by him reading her thoughts. He managed to hold back another round of laughter until he was alone in the hallway.

****

When she'd locked herself in, she finally broke out in a laugh. A quick shower later and she was ready for work. Downstairs, a taxi waited when she arrived. The doorman told her Tony had asked him to have one waiting for her at ten. Vaughn thanked the man and tried to be mad at Tony. Instead, she found it hard not to let her lips curl into a smile. These little things reminded her how he loved her and understood her need for space while doing his best to keep her safe. He was giving her her independence but not letting go.

Work was a relief. The simple repetitive tasks kept her mind busy. Her music choices tonight were light, an evening of songs famous from Broadway musicals. She cued up the waltz from *Carousel* and then a familiar version of "If I Loved You."

By the time her shift was over, she reasoned the love songs she'd played all night were in direct correlation to her emotional uproar. How could she love Tony so much and be willing to let him go so easily?

It was the thought she fell asleep with when her exhausted body and mind finally caved in the next morning. Her tormented dreams hadn't allowed her to sleep peacefully, even though she couldn't remember them when she woke.

Chapter Fifteen

Tony didn't want to be away from Vaughn, but his quick errand was worth the time and effort. He'd called in a few old favors and flown to Texas the next morning. He met Greer at an office downtown, which he had assumed was a front until he arrived. The bustling reception area was lavish, not what he was expecting. His eight-minute wait had given him time to accept the coffee offered him by a middle-aged male assistant. He'd sipped at it, enjoying the fresh brew after airline coffee.

When he was finally shown into a conference room at the far end of the hallway, he knew the choice of room was to impress him. The burled wood table would easily accommodate twenty people. The lush carpet swallowed up his feet as his eyes glanced at the art hung on the walls. He recognized some of the artists' works and found Mr. Hal Greer watching him from a side door.

Their appointment was surreal in many ways. He didn't know what to expect of the other man, but short, rotund, and balding wasn't it. He was dressed in an expensive dark blue suit, the cut minimizing his girth. His silk tie was Hermes, and his shoes handmade Italian leather.

"Impressive, isn't it?" Mr. Greer asked. He moved easily for a man of his weight, his right hand coming forward to shake Tony's.

"Quite impressive."

"Have a seat, Mr. Lombardo, or should I still call you 'Detective'?" This was Greer's way of letting him know he knew why he was there. "Before you let your imagination run wild, I have sales receipts for everything hanging in the room."

"I'm retired, Mr. Greer. Thank you for seeing me on such short notice." He waited until the other man took a seat, surprised he chose the center of the long table, not the head.

Tony pulled out the chair beside him and dropped into it. For a long pause, they sized each other up before Tony finally got down to business. "I'm here because a friend of mine has been having some problems, and I wondered if there might be a way to...end her harassment."

Hal Greer sat back in his seat, a large smile forming on his thick lips. At ease in his situation, Tony decided. He seemed to be straightforward with him so far. Relieving the onus of misdoings by him and his company would be advantageous to his business.

"Mr. Lombardo, I know Vivian is your lover, and I've recently been apprised of the harassment she's been experiencing. I've nothing to do with it. In reality, she did me a favor. Reno and I are cousins. We were both left half a business by our grandfather. By her taking Reno out of the picture, I've been able to step in and turn the entire business legitimate, something I'd tried to do for years. Just ask the IRS. We pay more taxes these days than ever before. All our companies are run strictly, and we have several outside auditing firms to keep everyone honest. I don't know who's making trouble, but I have nothing to do with it."

"Yet you just admitted you knew where she was and the problems she was having."

"Only since your call to set up this appointment. Yes, it pays to keep up with these sorts of details."

"She's not a detail, damn it. She's..."

"The woman you love, Detective?" His laugh was hearty, genuine. "Mr. Lombardo, if I'd wanted Vivian out of the way, it would have been handled long before this. I hold no animosity against her, as I said earlier. She did me a favor."

"Do you have any idea who's behind the terrorizing?"

"No, but I could look into it if you'd like?"

Tony stood so quickly his chair almost toppled over behind him. "No, thank you." He sat back down, knowing he'd overacted. "I'm just trying to eliminate some of the more public details, shall we say?"

"I think she's given up enough of her life to put Reno behind bars. I've no quarrel with her. I feel it's about time she had a real life and started enjoying it."

"Then I should thank you for your time and let you get back to business."

"All right, but there's one thing I can help with." He looked Tony in the eyes. "Reno doesn't have the means to do this anymore, not that I know of. He's nothing more than a communal wet nurse these days and will continue to be for the rest of his life. If he's behind it, it's with the help of someone other than his old buddies. As to Mike Elder, he's never carried the clout."

"Thank you for your honesty." He stood and shook Greer's hand.

"I have nothing against her or her parents. Should they want to leave Arizona or spend time with their daughter, I'm not going to interfere."

"Thank you." Tony tried to keep his features noncommittal. He tasted fear in a new direction if Hal Greer was telling the truth and a bit of relief at the same time.

"One last thing, Mr. Lombardo."

Tony turned with his hand on the doorknob, almost afraid to hear what might come.

"If you marry her, it wouldn't bother me or any of my known associates. She doesn't pose a threat to any of us, understand?"

"Yes, I do."

"Good. Consider the information a wedding present from Greer and Co."

Tony slid out the door, his hands suddenly clammy and damp. He forced himself to walk calmly to the elevator and not to acknowledge the receptionist. Even in the elevator, he forced himself to hold his composure.

Only outside in the humid Texas air, miles from the building, did he pull into a gas station and hit the men's room. He splashed water on his face and looked in the warped mirror above the sink. He wasn't sure what he was seeing, but he knew his future held Vaughn in a prominent place.

Even though Daniels had said he'd check the Texas connections, he had to do this interview for himself. It was okay to trust others sometimes, but not this time.

With the pressure off her from Greer, he could concentrate his efforts back in Manhattan. It didn't give him a place to start really. It just eliminated places to be checked. The drive back to the airport seemed endless. He called Daniels on his cell and told him about his meeting.

Daniels wasn't happy about his confrontation with Greer, but Daniels wasn't happy with most anything Tony did. The flight back to LaGuardia was long, and he finally fell asleep. When he awoke upon touchdown, his head ached and his stomach churned. At least he was on his home territory.

****

Chester Daniels had been right. Nothing made sense in Vaughn's case. Tony had treated it like one of his cold cases, starting at the beginning and reading each interview, court document, and report he could gather. At first, he'd been surprised when Daniels obtained the files. He realized he was doing it for Vaughn. Daniels would assist him, leaving his personal feelings aside.

Three weeks later, he knew every page by heart, but something was missing. There had to be, unless it was simply a crazed person who attached themselves to Vaughn from her radio job.

He had taken to staying up all night lately listening to her shows. He'd adopted her schedule, sleeping in the mornings. Somehow it made him feel in sync with her, even if she was pushing him farther and farther away.

There hadn't been any incidents at her apartment, and now that renovations were almost finished, he waited patiently for her to move back in. He'd offered to help her, but she was adamant that she only had some clothes to bring over and she wanted to take care of it herself. He'd taken a step back and left her alone.

His sudden back-off approach seemed to confuse her. When she first put distance between them, it drove him crazy. He wanted to pull her up hard against his body and kiss some sense into her. He hadn't. He'd accepted her words and acted upon her wishes—for now.

He believed she'd never let him close until she was sure she was safe, and he didn't fight her. He turned his mind to the case, hoping to find out who was harassing her and why. Only after that was resolved could he expect to talk to her rationally again.

****

Vaughn stood in the center of her living room. Its shiny white walls and glossy trim seemed almost virginal. Maybe that was why she told the painter to change the color. The apricot would bring back memories, and she wanted a fresh start. She'd start at the beginning and build a life for herself.

"It all sounds great," she said aloud in the empty room, reminding herself how hard it was to start again. But she would. There was no other choice except to run, and that she wouldn't do.

The new furniture was due to be delivered tomorrow, but her new bed had arrived. The large brass headboard was swirled with graceful curves that formed side rails and ran to the footboard. She'd changed the placement of the furniture, and with its white walls, this room looked different too. Solid white panels of linen covered the french doors into the space. Privacy with light had been that deciding factor. It still creeped her out to know somebody had watched her and Tony have sex.

The marshals had found an empty apartment in the

building across the street. They'd concluded someone had slipped in without notice and used the space to spy on her and Tony. No one had contacted them that the tenant had moved out. They assumed whoever had used the apartment had a telescope or a camera with a long lens. Thankfully, no photos had been found.

She pulled the new sheets from the laundry wrap and proceeded to make her new bedroom livable. The maroon-and-green-floral comforter complemented the striped sheets and throw pillows. Solid maroon curtains hung over white sheer panels, giving the room a punch of color.

She'd started collecting small wreaths of dried flowers and had tacked them along the ceiling line like a border. She took a breath and looked around her new bedroom. It was definitely different from before. That goal had been accomplished. The colors were more winter than summer, and she didn't care. Her newly refurbished wardrobe hung neatly in her closet.

****

Vaughn was taking her new white dishes from the dishwasher and stacking them in the cabinet when her intercom rang. It was strange because she wasn't expecting any deliveries or company. Gus told her one of the marshals was on his way up to see her.

She moved cautiously to the apartment door. Daniels always called her before he came by. A chill of fear ran down her spine when there was a knock on the door. She froze at first and then hollered at the door, "Be right there," before detouring to her phone and hitting the preset for Daniels's cell. She got his voicemail and left a message confirming the appearance of the marshal.

The knock on the door got louder, and she grabbed the dish towel from the counter before going to it. Through the peephole she could only see a man. His dark suit and short hair were obscured by thick glasses and a mustache. He waited very close to the door, making any real identification almost impossible. Again, he knocked. This time it was louder because she was leaning against the inside of it.

"Yes, who is it?" she called through the door.

"Agent Travers, Ms. Matthews. Agent Daniels asked me to bring by these papers for you. He said it was important." He waited while she absorbed the information.

"He didn't call me about them." She stalled for time, hoping the cell phone in her hand would ring.

"Yes, ma'am. He said you should call him as soon as you get this information. He's tied up."

A strange lilt in the man's voice set her on edge. "I'm not dressed. Could you just leave them on the floor for me, and I'll get them in a few minutes? This is really bad timing." She watched through the small viewer as he stood there for a while, looking at the envelope in his hand. She wished he'd move back so she could see who he was. It became a moot point seconds later when he spoke again.

"Ms. Matthews, I'll leave the envelope by your door, but it's important you see these as soon as possible. Please don't forget to take them."

"As soon as I'm dressed, Agent Travers."

"Yes, ma'am." He moved away from the door, and Vaughn lost sight of him. She knew not to open the door and tried Daniels's number again. This time she left another brief message. "Daniels, I got the papers you sent. They said I was supposed to call you. Where are you?" Why hadn't he answered the phone? It was an extension of his arm most times. "Okay, I guess you're not there. Call me back."

Vaughn checked the hallway as well as she could through the peephole before she opened the door. She opened it a few inches, leaving the chain on just in case. Her arm snaked out through the opening to take the papers. Once they were in her grasp, she moved back quickly and secured herself inside.

The large brown envelope was heavier than she'd expected. She walked back to the kitchen, unclasped it, and let the pages fall on the counter in front of her. She forgot to breathe when she saw what littered the surface. Black-and-white photographs of her were blown up to eight by tens.

There were candid shots of her from the first day she'd come to Manhattan. There were ones from the day she ran home in the thunderstorm, her hair plastered to her head, her makeup running down her cheeks. Tony and Daniels were in a few as well.

"Oh my God," she whispered as it suddenly all came together. Whoever was watching her was very thorough. There were shots of her coming and going from her new apartment as well as the hotel she'd just left. At the bottom of the pile were shots of both spaces, her personal items prominent.

"He's been in the hotel too." She let herself get used to the idea of her space being violated once again. The last pictures bothered her the most. Taken through the openings in the blinds were ones of her and Tony lying in bed together. The photographs progressed through their morning of lovemaking, ending with her hand touching his shoulder.

That very evening Tony had told her about being shot. It had brought them closer together. He'd told her the honest truth that night. "I retired before I died. Sheer self-preservation made my decision. I'm not sorry about it. Getting shot was a reality check. I wanted a stable life."

He'd also told her he wanted her to be a part of it.

Knowing now he would never be a part of her life, she let the tears flow. She'd never be rid of the past. Her fate was to be alone until whoever this was chose to end her days. The idea made her mad. She wanted more from her life, had earned more after giving up all these years to do the right thing.

She hadn't heard him enter the kitchen so much as felt his presence. The door swung open soundlessly, but a rustle of air caught her attention.

"How did you get in?" she asked without turning around. The jangle of keys behind her soured her stomach. This would be her final showdown. Her life hung in the balance. Tony's face smiled up at her from the counter, and she drew her finger along his lips, the taste of him forming in her mind. "What do you want from me?"

"Everything…" the male voice said. Its sound was familiar.

Dread coursed through her body. "Greer promised me this was over."

"I don't work for Greer. I'm independent."

"Who pays you and why?"

"Not in my contract to say."

His cocky attitude annoyed her, but she wouldn't let the bastard get her. She would outthink him and maybe stay alive. "Since it's my life hanging in the balance, I would think I'd have a right to know."

"I don't renege on contracts. I finish the job I was paid to do."

"Who paid you?" The long silence behind her wasn't good. There were no utensils in the drainboard, and the block with her knives was at the far end of the counter. Any movement and he'd see. Then it struck her. He'd been on the team fixing her door after the break-in, the man who wouldn't meet her gaze.

"Would you like a cup of coffee?" she asked.

His sinister laugh behind her made her jump. The telephone ringing on the counter sent her into overdrive, but he reached it before she could. The gloved hand pulled the unit from the table and pushed the power button. Now she was shut off from the world—and what life might have been. Her only regret was that she'd pushed Tony away.

****

Tony ducked out of the cab and under the awning before the large drops of rain could dampen him. Gus pulled open the inner door. "Thanks, what's going on today? I thought it was supposed to be sunny and warm."

"That's what they predicted. This is just a passing spring shower." Gus winked.

"Is that what you call it?" he joked as he waited for the elevator to arrive.

"It will be a few minutes. One of the marshals went up to see Ms. Matthews a few minutes ago."

Tony turned to Gus. Something didn't feel right. "One of the marshals, not Daniels?"

"No, this one I met when their team came in to

clean up." The expression on Gus's face changed when he digested Tony's statement.

Tony dropped his groceries in front of the elevator and headed for the stairs, dragging off his jacket and letting it fall behind him as he went. Halfway up the first flight of stairs, he paused to pull a small revolver from his ankle holster.

"Gus, call Daniels. Tell him to get over here. Something's not right."

"But his identification was all in order, and I remembered him from the team who put in the alarm and cameras."

Tony hesitated, and it finally all became clear. "Get hold of Daniels, and get him here just in case." He took the rest of the flight two steps at a time. He didn't let the smell on two bother him. Instead, he used it to propel him up to the next flight. He reached the fourth-floor landing and paused to check the hallway. Hearing a noise behind him, he turned and saw Daniels putting less distance between them. He waited at the top of the landing.

"That was quick," Tony said.

"What's going on? Vaughn left several messages about some papers I never sent. Why are you here with a gun drawn?"

It had been a few weeks since they'd seen or talked to each other. He took a moment to stare at Daniels, and it reinforced their bond to take care of Vaughn. "Gus said one of your men came by with an envelope. Said his ID checked out, so he let him up. Also said he recognized him from the alarm team."

"The alarm team? They wouldn't be running errands. Shit!" Daniels said.

"My sentiments exactly. You wearing a vest?" Tony asked.

"No." He glanced at Tony, who wasn't wearing one either.

"She's home alone with a crazy man. I can't not go in." Tony took a few tentative steps.

"I have a spare set of keys. Let's just keep our cool until we know what's really happening."

He knew Daniels was trying to be rational, but right now he only felt anger and fear. "And give him more time with her? Forget it. I'm going in. Call for backup."

"Don't get in a snit," Daniels whispered. "I already did, and you're not going in alone. We do this as a team."

"Agreed. See if she answers her phone?"

Daniels punched numbers and waited, holding it away from his ear for Tony to hear the immediate voicemail message.

"All right, I go to the door as if I'm expected. You get ready to—"

"Yeah, yeah, just get going."

They moved slowly down the corridor, each man on one side of the hallway. When they reached the end, Tony drew a deep breath and knocked loudly. "Vaughn, I'm home, hon. I forgot my key." He raised a shoulder to Daniels, who only raised an eyebrow in return. Tony tried again and then a third time. When he still got no answer, Daniels came forward and opened the locks with amazing patience to stifle the noise.

Tony coughed loudly each time the tumblers clanked. He took a step back and motioned to Daniels. He punched a wrong code into the keypad, knowing it would set off the alarm when he opened the door.

He tried the knob, but it wouldn't budge. Finally, he lost his patience. With one strong kick of his leg, the door swung open. Daniels came in low, and Tony took high. The living room was empty, and the french doors were open to the bedroom. The window and the iron gate to the fire escape were open.

"Vaughn?" he called.

Daniels went through to the bedroom while Tony detoured into the kitchen. He found her slumped on the floor. As he ran his hands along her body, he hollered to Daniels to get help. When he didn't come up with any blood, he sat beside her, checking her pulse a second time. There was a dark mark on her cheek where she'd been struck. He pulled her up against his chest. "Wake up, angel. You can come back. You're safe now, and you're not alone."

****

Vaughn roused from the dark tunnel and thought she heard Tony's voice. But it couldn't be—she'd sent him away. She came awake when she remembered the man in her apartment. She fought Tony's arms around her until his voice penetrated her fear.

"It's all right, Vaughn. I've got you." He repeated it until she was able to focus on him. "You're all right."

She'd never thought to be in his arms again and let her arms move around his waist, pulling him to her. "He was here," she finally managed to say.

Daniels entered the kitchen and sized up the situation. "Bedroom's clear. You okay?" he asked her. He didn't wait for an answer. Instead, he moved around them and went to the pictures littering the counter.

"Let's get you off the floor," Tony said, and

Daniels reached to help her up.

After heading to Tony's apartment, she sat heavily on the tan couch. He pressed a dish towel wrapped around ice cubes into her hand to hold against her cheek. He left momentarily and returned with coffee in mugs for all three of them.

"Can you talk to us?" Daniels asked, apparently unsure how fragile she was at that moment.

"Can I talk to you? That son of a bitch has been following me from the day I set foot here. How did this happen? How could you allow him on your team?" She was fired up, finally venting the anger and hostility she'd held in since realizing she was in trouble not of her doing once again. She tossed the rag on the table and stood, not caring that the ice cubes sputtered along the surface. She paced the length of the room.

Tony knew enough to sit back and give her some space, but Daniels seemed a little more shocked at her outburst.

"On my team? Do you know who he was, Vaughn?"

She stopped and stared, realizing he was totally unaware.

Tony leaned forward. "Got to be your old pal Williams, or whoever he really is."

"Who? I don't have a Williams on my team." Daniels shook his head.

"No, neither did Jacob. He was Reno's plant, the last-minute fill-in on the team who got called away. That left Marcus alone with Vaughn," Tony said.

She turned to him, surprised he'd put the pieces together. "Yes, that's right. How did you know?" She sat beside him, taking the rag and gathering the cubes before pressing it against her cheek once again.

"It was the only loose end. Greer claimed he didn't want you dead, and there were no stalkers we could identify in the city. He was the only loose end from your Reno days."

"Yes, he told me he never went back on a contract. He'd been paid, and he'd do the job. How did you figure it out?"

"Simple. I've spent the last weeks reviewing your case, looking at it through cold-case eyes. He was the only detail never accounted for."

"He said it was nothing personal, just his reputation on the line. He said it didn't look good for his credibility. A hit man with a live woman, a woman he hadn't been able to get. I think we hurt his pride." Vaughn said it with a laugh that broke the tension.

Tony's intercom rang, and when he returned, he told Daniels the team was on the way up. Maybe they could get prints from the window or grating. While all three of them doubted it, protocol was protocol. He hoped one of the men would be able to identify the stranger or at least give them a good description of the interloper.

****

The photos were laid out on the table in Tony's kitchen. Daniels muttered under his breath, looking annoyed that this had happened on his watch. It was obvious he took it as a personal insult. Vaughn let him work through the situation without interfering. He stared at the photos of them standing outside the new hotel. The camera caught his vulnerability, and she didn't remind him of the conversation they were having when the photos were taken.

At this very moment, questions were being asked at the marshals' office. Until they knew how "Williams," as they had taken to calling him, had infiltrated the team, Daniels wouldn't rest. They all agreed for the next few days, it would be quiet. Williams would have to regroup after failing once again.

"I know he's really going to be pissed the next time he comes after me." Her words took both men away from their separate thoughts.

"New plan, angel," Tony told her. "We're going to take you out of the equation."

"No plan, Tony. I am the equation. And he won't stop until we stop him. Daniels, can you get me a gun?"

Both men sat up in their chairs, looking to the other, then back at her.

"*No*. It's not a good idea under any circumstances." Daniels's tone told her those were his last words on the subject. "The statistics…"

"I know how to shoot. Jacob taught me years ago. I will not go quietly to my death. If he comes after me again, I'm going to shoot him before he kills me."

"No," Daniels told her again. "I'll not have blood on your hands."

"Fine," she shouted back. "I'll get one on my own."

"It's not a good idea, Vaughn." Daniels's tone was adamant.

She laughed at his stern look. "Fine, then get me another Taser. At least—"

"What do you mean another Taser?" Tony asked.

She looked at him with a mock smile. "I've had a Taser and pepper spray in my coat pocket the whole time I've been here. But I always leave them in my coat pocket. Not a good idea. So if you won't get me a gun legally, get me another Taser to keep in the apartment." She let out a sigh. "It's bad enough to have to carry that damn cell phone from room to room. Now I'll be carrying that and a Taser."

"What if this crazy man takes it from you?" Daniels's tone said more than his words.

"And what if he doesn't? It's the best idea I can come up with to protect myself."

"I don't like it," Daniels said as he paced the room.

"I don't like it either, but without a gun, it's all I've got to work with." She challenged him with her glare. "Unless you get me a small revolver."

"No guns." Daniels pulled out his phone and stepped to the far corner of the room, his conversation in hushed tones.

"Did you ever use the Taser?" Tony asked.

"Only for target practice when I was out west with Jacob. The same time he taught me to shoot. But when I moved to New York City with its strict laws, the Taser seemed a better fit." She stared at him. "It just doesn't help being in my coat!"

Daniels finished his phone call. "No guns," he repeated.

It became a staring contest between Daniels and Vaughn until Tony spoke up. "Settle down, boys and girls. Nobody is getting Vaughn a gun. I have a better idea." His input stopped their tense moment, and they both turned to look at him.

"What?" Her tone revealed her angst.

"Your job at the station ends this weekend. I know of an empty apartment in Brooklyn you can stay in for a few weeks." She started to protest, but he talked over her. "You can still get to the city during the day if you get voice work, but at night you'll be safe. Isn't that the main point of all of this?"

"I won't put your family in the middle of this."

"I know. I won't either." He laughed aloud, adding, "I'll put them on either side of you." He went on to explain about the second-floor apartment in the house next to his parents. Only temporary, he told her, until they could catch Williams. Their debate grew loud and then turned softer again.

"You'd never forgive me if something happened to your family, and I'd never forgive myself. No, I'll take my chances here. We'll re-alarm, relock, and put cameras in the hallway and on the fire escape. Hell, get a hallway camera that shows up on my phone. I won't be forced out again." Asserting her independence, she left them sitting in Tony's apartment while she went back to hers.

She was thankful they didn't follow her. She needed these few minutes alone to gather her thoughts and courage, although she wouldn't admit the courage side. She needed to wall off her emotions to get through the night.

Tony had kicked in the door, but only the chain was damaged. The alarms and locks were intact. She busied herself wiping away print dust from the window and doorknobs and changed for work. Her cheek and eye throbbed, but she'd be damned if she'd run again. Three aspirin and some heavy makeup later, she was ready to leave for work.

She didn't utter a word when Daniels slid beside her in the back of the taxi. Not a word in the elevator. When she was in the studio, she looked at him and with a nod, closed the door, and made sure it was locked.

She couldn't have talked to him. Even a thank-you would be forced. While this wasn't his fault, or hers or Tony's, she couldn't find the words. The reality was Reno had hired an inept hit man who was obviously pissed off his reputation was on the line.

Deep breaths forced her to control the overwhelming emotions, and she went to the console, temporarily losing herself in the process.

She still had uneasy feelings. Williams was probably listening and seething at his miss. The next time would be their last confrontation. It would be him or her. Time would tell. She could only hope she'd win. Vaughn took the Taser from her coat pocket and slid it into her pants pocket. The pepper spray she'd leave in her coat as a backup. Neither item had done her any good hanging on the coatrack. From now on she'd carry the Taser from room to room, as she did with her phone. She promised herself on the way home she'd stop to get extra canisters of spray and hide them in each room where she could get to them easily.

Chapter Sixteen

Vaughn was leaving her apartment less and less. At first, she'd told herself it was because she had no place to go. A lie, she knew. There was always something to do in Manhattan. From movies to museums, she could have found something besides daytime television. It could become addictive: which soap character lied to whom about who the baby's real father was, which talk show had the better guests and who made her laugh. At this time in her life, her only connections to the outside world were through world news, game shows, and weekly dramas.

She hated that Williams was winning the psychological war, hated that she waited for him to decide her fate. Instinct told her he might try to ambush her outside the next time. Even with her pockets full of tricks, she still felt safer at home.

Instead, she had locked herself away in the air-conditioned rooms that were rapidly becoming her new prison. For two months, Daniels and Tony had searched for Williams. They learned he'd been a last-minute replacement to the team when one of the regulars was injured in a "convenient" fender bender that very morning. He'd slipped in virtually unnoticed, his fake identification assuring him access.

They'd discovered there was a real agent Williams, Timothy Williams, who was a lawyer in the

Washington, DC, office. When routine checks were made, everything came back to the real Williams, and everyone assumed it was a transfer, just as all the papers had said. However, he was in his sixties and about to retire. He had no idea his identity had been stolen.

She'd spoken with Jacob, but she was pulling away from him too. He'd wanted her to come back to Seattle if only for a few weeks. She'd refused. Although her parents were on alert, she tried to calm their fears with her weekly telephone call.

Daniels checked on her every other day by phone and still asked her out to supper or coffee each time. The invitations weren't romantic anymore. She felt as if he were an older brother keeping watch on her. Tony had pulled back too. She'd chased him away with harsh words and crude accusations they both knew weren't true.

Every time she thought of something to do outside, she would remember the pictures. Running in the park, working out at her health club, wandering Madison Avenue. When she did venture out, she went with a strict list of errands, never to be varied from; only the route she took changed each time. She watched over her shoulder all the time now and knew she couldn't live like this. Her inner debate was whether to go underground on her own or ask Daniels for help. Knowing Williams had twice infiltrated their tight sector, she was hesitant to go back. She hated that state of limbo she was in and grabbed her purse. It was a now-or-never moment.

On a beautiful spring afternoon, she left the building in a hurry and disappeared into the lunchtime crowds. On the subway she knew her general destination. Vaughn found herself wandering the small area of Brooklyn Tony had grown up in. The rows of brick homes, all neatly laid out in grid patterns, were comforting. The local shops that were frequented by neighborhood residents were her favorite. She ate slices of pizza at the counter of Vito's and wandered through the sale racks of the small clothing shops.

It was dark when she left what could become her favorite shop. The owner was about her age and had a playpen in the corner behind her desk. She carried basic classic clothing with a few novelty sweaters thrown in. Vaughn instantly liked the rock music that filtered through the small store. She liked the easy conversation over her choice of earrings. With her small purchase tucked away in her purse, she bid farewell to the very pregnant owner after shaking the chubby toddler's hand. As she turned at the corner to get her bearings, she walked right into Tony. His mouth slid into an easy smile, one she almost reached up to kiss.

"What are you doing here?" she asked, trying to keep anger over arousal in her tone.

"I used to live here, remember? I could ask you the same thing." He leaned his weight on his right hip and watched her.

He made her nervous in that sensual way her body remembered. Just the scent of him had her nipples budding and her body heating. God, she missed him, in her life and especially in her bed. Again, she almost reached out to him. "I was shopping."

"In Brooklyn, three blocks from my parents' house?"

"Yes," she said defensively. "I walked down here

with your dad that morning and wanted to come back when the shops were open." She stood in a hard stance, her feet planted shoulder-width apart, her head high, her eyes narrowed.

He looked at her and started to laugh. It was a laugh she missed. Finally, she relaxed her shoulders and gave him a half smile. The absurd thing was that deep down, she'd come to Brooklyn to see how she felt here. Unfortunately, she felt comfortable. This was a place she could live. Knowing it didn't make the situation any better, especially after running into Tony. In reality, it made the situation worse because she could never really live here without him. She pulled in a deep breath. There had to be other towns and cities and neighborhoods similar to this. She'd find one where the love of her life didn't live.

Vaughn knew a lot of things about herself. First and foremost, she'd fallen in love with Tony. She believed he'd fallen in love with her too, which meant she had to move on, or he'd never be safe. Nor would his family. No amount of hubris could stop a pissed-off killer with a knife or bullet. Williams and his vendetta would come. If he couldn't get her, he'd take out one of Tony's family to terrorize all of them.

She stared into his brown eyes and melted inside. She had to detach herself from the moment. "I have to get back to the city."

"Can I give you a lift?"

"Yes." There was no hesitation in her voice. She'd missed him, missed being around him. She'd mourned his loss in her own way every day. She refused to toss aside the minutes they could spend together. One last memory, she told herself, to take with her, to always remember him. While she would have liked to screw his brains out a few more times, that wouldn't help her leave him. For now, she'd accept the ride back to the city.

She was quiet when they started back. She didn't ask him why he was in Brooklyn the same time she was. Then she remembered she thought she'd seen Carmen. She'd ducked into the bakery, but now it didn't matter. It was a small community, and in reality, everyone knew if someone belonged. She longed to have that feeling again, to be a part of a community.

"Carmen called you? I'll assume you had my phone GPS all along, so you've known where I was." She released a deep breath. "I wonder if Williams has my GPS information too."

He gave her a quick shoulder shrug. She decided he hadn't considered that option and wasn't willing to open the conversation right now.

"I was here helping Dad fix the lawn mower."

"Oh."

Back in the city, they walked the short distance from the parking garage to their building. Gus was on vacation, and they both greeted Patrick. They automatically headed to the stairs, hurrying through the second-floor lobby. Vaughn stopped, and Tony backtracked to her side.

"I've got it. It's perfume that's soured!" She threw her arms around his neck and let out a yell of relief.

He lost his balance with her surprise launch at him.

"I don't know who dropped gallons of it, but that's the smell, Tony."

"Well, how do we get rid of it?" he teased. "I guess we'll just have to accept it will always be part of the

205

building." He took her hand, and they wandered slowly up the next flight.

"I don't know. How long have you lived here?"

Their light banter continued until they reached the fourth-floor lobby. At the far end, something large sat on the floor, leaning against her door.

"Stay here," he barked. He made his way slowly down the hall.

She objected and followed him. He drew his gun before seeing what was there. With her close behind, he stopped dead in the center of the hallway.

"It's Williams!" She wandered past Tony to get a better view. Williams sat on the floor, his ankles cuffed together. His hands were cuffed behind his back. Silver duct tape was wrapped around his upper body and his legs from knees to ankles. Another strip was placed across his mouth.

Pinned to his chest was the largest white-ribbon bow she'd ever seen outside a car showroom, with an envelope pinned to it. She reached for it, but Tony's arm came out in front of her. She hesitated, wanted to object, but took a step back away from Williams.

His beady eyes stared at her, and she was revolted by the look of him. The last time he'd caught her, he'd blatantly told her how he would abuse her before killing her. The memory of his words turned her stomach.

Tony's and Daniels's intervention had been the only thing that saved her. The timing had been flawless, or they might have found her in a totally different predicament. Anger washed over her, and she stepped back. The urge to kick him surprised her. She wanted to physically hurt him, which was a first for her.

Tony patted him down for weapons and found

none. "Here." He thrust his phone at her. "Call Daniels and take some stills. Don't touch him. I want to get a picture of this," he told her before disappearing into his apartment. He returned with a small digital camera and shot some video. Then he took shots of the bound-and-gagged man from all angles.

He turned and saw her standing with her Taser in her hand. "Don't, Vaughn."

"Why? For everything he's done to me, why can't I get in one shot or at least one jolt? Come on, Tony. Tell me you don't have the urge to kick him in the balls or at least the kidneys."

"Actually, I do, but at this point in my life, I've learned control."

"Do me a favor and go back inside your apartment for just a minute." She all but stared him down with the hope he might leave her. He didn't move.

"It won't make you feel better, hon. Momentarily, yes, but long term, you'll just feel crappy."

"I'll take crappy if I can watch him squirm in pain, even if it is only temporary." They watched the bound man squirm more, trying to talk through his gag. "Fuck me, I hate it when you play on my conscience. Just take your pictures." She slipped the Taser back in her pocket.

Tony turned on the unit a second time and let it run for several minutes until they heard noise on the stairs.

Daniels's voice reached them before his body did. "Vaughn." He rounded the top of the stairs and stopped dead, apparently not believing what he saw. He made his way down the hall, tucking his gun away as he did. "What the hell is going on here?"

"Don't know. We just got here when we called

you." Tony glanced at Vaughn and shook his head. "Better him to explain to the cops than us."

"The police are on the way, and so is the rest of my team," Daniels said.

"Should we unwrap him?" Vaughn asked, her laughter bubbling up from pent-up anxiety. "Or should we put him in the closet until next Christmas, like an old fruitcake?" She sobered when she realized all three men were staring. "I'd like to see what's on the note."

Tony reached forward and took the straight pin from the ribbon. He handed the envelope to her. She felt it in her hands for a moment before sliding her finger under the glued tab and tugging out a small white card on thick stock.

She read the words carefully several times before sharing them with Tony and Daniels. "A wedding present." There were no other identifying marks. "Who did this and how?" She looked from Tony to Daniels.

"Maybe Hal Greer," Tony mused aloud.

Daniels only shook his head.

She and Daniels turned to look at him. "Why? He claimed he had no interest in me," Vaughn said.

"He probably doesn't. But a hit man on the loose after you probably made him uncomfortable. Reno will probably be relieved too. Williams might have information Reno doesn't want going public for more charges." Tony shrugged. "Daniels, what do you think?"

"I think we all agree there was no card."

His stern look had Vaughn and Tony nodding in acknowledgment.

They decided it had to have been Hal Greer. He had finally caught up with Williams, or whatever his real name turned out to be.

Tony slipped the card into his pocket as the noise of the arriving police cars made its way up the stairs. "No note, agreed?" He turned to Daniels, who nodded. Vaughn understood. Tony took several more photos without the card. Daniels took several on his phone.

"How did Mr. Greer do this?" she asked both men. They looked at each other and gave a similar shrug. "Aren't you curious? You both spent so much time trying to find him, and Hal Greer did it." She wanted an answer. She hated loose ends.

"We're not sure it was Greer. In fact, we have no evidence in that direction. Angel, I think this is one thread we shouldn't pull. Sometimes you just snip them off and accept the hitch in the weave." Tony's arm dropped over her shoulder. "Daniels, what do you think?"

"I'm thinking along the same lines as you. We let this end of it go and focus on how Williams infiltrated the DC office and computers and got the identification documents. Then we can see what other contract hits and security breaches he's responsible for." Daniels smiled. "DNA is a wonderful thing, especially when you consider cold cases from years ago. Not many madmen wore gloves back then."

A garbled moan came from the man on the floor, one that didn't need verification. Just the idea of Daniels tracking his past would make Williams antsy.

"Tony's right, Vaughn. We let this thread go and work with the knowns. Bringing up the unknowns will hurt someone in the end." He gave her a lopsided smile. "How often have you heard me say he was right? Let's just let this be a vague moment. In the long run, you're safe now. That's what matters."

****

Tony introduced the two patrolmen who responded to Vaughn's and Daniels's calls. It was Daniels who took care of getting Williams from their hallway when his team arrived. While both officers obviously wanted to ask how their arrest had gotten there and who had tied and cuffed him, they apparently sensed it was better not to know when the marshals flashed their badges. The marshals' laughter at the man's predicament had their prisoner's face turning redder and redder.

"I've got to go and take care of this. I want to make sure he's held someplace secure, without bail."

"Thank you, Chester," Vaughn whispered, reaching up to place a small kiss on his cheek.

He blushed at the attention. "I've got work to do," he grumbled.

The agents had the man on his feet but hadn't cut the tape or uncuffed him. The bindings forced Williams to bunny hop down the hall. Tony and Vaughn let out a roaring laugh at the sight.

Sobering, Tony stared at her. "Are we okay?"

"I hope so. I love you too much to lose you again." Her hand went to his face, tugging him toward her lips.

****

Hours later lying sated against Tony, Vaughn finally asked, "Am I supposed to write Mr. Greer a thank-you note?"

"Let's just invite him to the wedding."

"Do you think he'd come?"

"You never know." He pulled her back under the covers with him.

****

Vaughn stood tall on her father's arm while he walked her down the aisle of the Brooklyn church Tony's family had belonged to for three generations. Carmen's children would be the fourth generation, as would hers and Tony's. The idea of permanence thrilled her.

Tony waited at the altar with Daniels beside him. Both men were dressed in black tuxedos. Carmen stood beside her in a black dress. Vaughn wore her mother's wedding gown, a simple sheath of candlelight satin with princess lines. She'd had a seamstress design a matching lace jacket with a high collar and long, straight sleeves.

A ring of fresh flowers held Tony's mother's veil, Vaughn's something borrowed, in place. The sunset ceremony was attended by only immediate family and friends, more people than Vaughn could imagine as being immediate. But she loved them all, and now she would be a part of them.

It seemed ages ago that her life had been so screwed up. "Williams," as they'd called him, turned out to have been using the real Tim Williams's identification for years. When the marshals had time to delve into his background, they found he was a wanted man in several states, all for murder-for-hire schemes. The marshals assumed he'd never see the light of day as a free man again.

Daniels had talked to Hal Greer, who claimed no knowledge of the incident, only relief that it was over for Vaughn. He hadn't pressed the point. Vaughn decided there were some things she was better off not knowing. She would let it go, along with the wonder of who shut down the recently installed exterior cameras for just the six minutes when Williams arrived on her doorstep. In her mind, there was no question—he had been on the installation team.

She'd sent Mr. Greer a wedding invitation and on it wrote a short note thanking him for her future.

On a crisp fall night, she and Tony exchanged vows with strong voices and clear hearts. Their kiss was anything but church-like, Tony taking her in his arms and letting her know she was his forever.

Dani and Helen were there as well as Gus and his wife. Jacob had made the journey too, his black eye patch a badge of his courage to Vaughn. She'd thought about going back to using Vivian, but Viv was long gone, and Vaughn was alive and well and marrying the man of her dreams. This was who she was, Vaughn Matthews Lombardo.

While they were outside taking photos with the wedding party, a black limousine sat across the street. Tony pulled a deep breath when he saw the unfamiliar vehicle and tightened his hold on Vaughn until he saw who emerged from the back seat. With a purposeful stride, the man crossed the street to greet them.

He extended his hand and shook both Tony's and Vaughn's hands. "My flight was late. I apologize. But it looks like you got the deed accomplished."

"Yes, thanks to some help from friends," Vaughn answered. She'd never met him, but she didn't need an introduction. "And thank you again for your generous wedding present."

"Not generous, just right for everyone involved."

"Giving Tony and me our future is generous. I thank you every night in my prayers."

"I can't stay. I'm on my way to meet my family out on Long Island. Have a good life." He kissed Vaughn lightly on each cheek.

She held him close for a moment longer. "Thank you for my future," she whispered. When she pulled back, she thought she saw tears in his eyes.

He walked away without turning back, only putting up one hand to wave goodbye. Neither of them acknowledged Greer's well-chosen words. "Not generous, just right for everyone involved."

They turned back to smile at their guests gathering on the church steps.

Vaughn wasn't sure how they'd become so lucky, but decidedly they were due. She was finding voice work with regularity and was in contract talks to be the voice of a new cartoon superwoman. Tony teased her it was a natural part for her to play. In her downtime, she worked at the dress shop while Teresa recovered from the delivery of her younger child. The job suited her, and so did the hours and the neighborhood people she met there. She and Teresa mused that Vaughn's babies could use the playpen in the corner too.

They were renting the second-floor apartment in Mrs. B's home. They had an agreement with her that when she decided to move to Florida, they would buy the house. They had also decided that when they were back from their honeymoon, they'd sell Vaughn's apartment and keep Tony's. There were too many memories in her apartment, and she could redecorate his beige rooms to her liking. That way they'd have an office to work from in the city.

Beyond that, she and Tony were working on another cold case together. With this one, the result was already known. A woman had been murdered for no apparent reason. Her body was found in the trunk of an abandoned vehicle on a state roadway.

Seven years had gone by with no movement on the case. The victim's aging father had contacted Tony about finding a resolution before he passed. They'd taken the case, given no work would be done until they returned from their month in Italy. There were family members to meet and a new country to explore. They'd have their honeymoon and set to work finding out who strangled and then dumped twenty-two-year-old Margaret Monahan.

Tony pulled her from the thought. "Are you ready to party for a while, Mrs. Lombardo?" He nipped at her earlobe as he whispered and then ran his tongue along her throat. Her body responded, and she turned from the crowd and held tight to Tony. It was a surreal moment for her, and she just wanted to take it all in, to make every moment a memory. This memory would be engrained. Standing in a bridal gown, pushing against her new husband's erection. When he dropped his arm lower, he cupped her buttocks and moved her over him.

Vaughn looked at the man she'd just married and thanked the powers all around her who helped get her to this point in life. He discreetly shifted her against him, and her body cried for his attention. But they had a once-in-a-lifetime celebration waiting, and she wanted everyone to enjoy it and have fun. Freedom was a marvelous drug.

"Absolutely, Mr. Lombardo." She gave him a coy smile. "Are you ready for afterward, husband?"

"Oh, Vaughn, you have no idea how ready I am." His kiss was a hard smack on her lips while he cupped her butt, teasing both of them into a long, slow frenzy that would have to wait to be sated.

A word from the author...

Having been born and raised on Long Island, New York, my husband and I were both eager to leave the urban lifestyle behind us and explore our futures. With his encouragement, I'm living my dream of writing romance novels full time. Our new rural setting allows us time to enjoy each other and leaves me guiltless hours in my imagination indulging my other passions.

www.cornellromance.com

Thank you for purchasing
this publication of The Wild Rose Press, Inc.

For questions or more information
contact us at
info@thewildrosepress.com.

The Wild Rose Press, Inc.
www.thewildrosepress.com

www.ingramcontent.com/pod-product-compliance
Lightning Source LLC
Chambersburg PA
CBHW070452260626
47161CB00004B/1280